'This good-lo
Daniel Henne

Sam turned with
looking forward to meeting you
potential friend.

As if drawn by a powerful magnet her eyes fell immediately on the tall dark-haired man standing just inside the room and Norman's words seemed to echo into infinity through the roaring in her head.

She had an impression of heat, as if something had splashed over her wrist and down onto her foot, and there was a distant sound as if china had shattered somewhere, but all she could see was a familiar pair of deep blue eyes.

She saw eyes like that every day when she looked at her son.

Daniel's eyes.

But this time they were in Daniel's face, and that was impossible because Daniel had died more than five years ago.

Dear Reader

A few months ago I was lucky enough to spend a week in Cumbria. While I was revisiting places I first came to know when our children were small, I found I was looking at them in a completely different way.

Suddenly the quaint little market town I'd once known so well was growing and turning into the background for a whole new cast of characters working in and around Denison Memorial Hospital. This book, my thirtieth Medical Romance™, is the first in a series of stories about those characters and I hope you enjoy reading about them as much as I enjoy creating them.

Perhaps along the way I can give you a taste of what it was like to live surrounded by such magnificent scenery and the inimitable Cumbrian people. I will certainly be going back again.

Happy reading.

Josie

COMING HOME
TO DANIEL

BY
JOSIE METCALFE

MILLS & BOON®

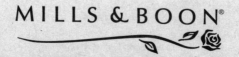

*First published in Great Britain 2001
Harlequin Mills & Boon Limited,
Eton House, 18-24 Paradise Road, Richmond, Surrey TW9 1SR*

© Josie Metcalfe 2001

ISBN 0 263 82667 8

*Set in Times Roman 10½ on 12 pt.
03-0601-47099*

*Printed and bound in Spain
by Litografia Rosés, S.A., Barcelona*

CHAPTER ONE

DANIEL HENNESSY deposited his bag beside the front door and strode on into the kitchen while he shrugged his way into his suit jacket.

'Well, Jamie, do you think you've remembered everything? Gym kit, school bag, lunch, shoes?'

'Dad! I don't forget things, now. I'm nearly six!' he protested with an indignant glare from deep blue eyes, then took another healthy bite of toast.

Daniel hid a smile behind his hand as he watched the youngster make short work of his breakfast, still amazed after all this time how much alike they were. It wasn't enough that they shared the same dark hair and deep blue eyes, but even the square jaw with a hint of a dimple was his own in miniature.

They also enjoyed their food and had a healthy dislike of being late which had meant an early agreement to work together in the mornings to get out of the house on time. If there had been a woman in their lives on a daily basis, things might have been easier on both of them, but he doubted they could have been organised any smoother.

Not that the only reason he might want a woman in their lives was to smooth out any wrinkles in their domestic arrangements. Although past experience had made him wary, he wasn't blinkered enough to deny that Jamie sometimes longed to have a mother figure in his life. God knew his grandmother tried her hardest, but with the best will in the world, a woman in her sixties wasn't able to keep up with an active five-going-on-six year old.

'Ready, Dad?' Jamie prompted with a pointed glance at the last bite of toast still hovering in mid-air as Daniel had stopped to muse. 'Don't forget to put your dirty things in the machine.'

'Cheeky!' He aimed a mock cuff at the taunting grin, but the youngster was too quick on his feet to stay in reach. 'Brush your teeth and grab your things. I'll be at the front door by the time you can count twenty.'

It was a game they'd started when he first went to school, Jamie learning to count as they both called the numbers aloud, hands busy while they collected their respective belongings.

'Nineteen, twenty. I was here first!' Jamie crowed as Daniel joined him in the hallway, keys at the ready. 'Have a good day,' he added in an oddly mature way while he flung his free arm around Daniel's waist, another little ritual instigated by a determinedly grown-up little boy who still needed a hug, but didn't want his friends to see.

'You have a good day, too,' Daniel said, giving him a squeeze and marvelling that he seemed to have grown another inch during the holidays. 'I expect your poor teacher will have a job keeping you all quiet while you catch up on everyone's news.'

'Wait till I tell her about dive-bombing you in the swimming pool,' he exclaimed as they made their way out to the car, harking back to one of their favourite outings during the school holidays. He'd been swimming like a fish almost before he could walk. 'And then I swam underneath you and caught your toe. Just think, Dad, if I'd been a shark, I could have eaten your leg off...'

'Mum! I can't find my shoes!' a despairing voice wailed from somewhere upstairs and Sam groaned.

'Neither can I,' she muttered as she gazed round at the half-unpacked boxes. 'This was obviously a very bad idea.'

It was her own fault that she was frantically trying to get her son ready for his first day at school and herself ready for work in a new job when she'd only arrived in the cottage yesterday.

To be fair, the practice had offered her a couple of days to get herself organised, but she was soft-hearted and knew how desperate they were with a key member of staff unexpectedly out of commission.

At this rate, it was going to take her a couple of days just to get the two of them dressed, and the last thing she wanted was to get her son off to a poor start on his first day.

Most of the time she was fairly well organised— well, as a single parent it was pretty essential, there certainly wasn't anyone else around to pick up the slack...

'Ah! Got them!' She pounced on the missing shoes. 'I *thought* I'd got them ready last night, but after that "talk" with Mother...'

She shook her head, refusing to relive yet another uncomfortable conversation about her shortcomings as a dutiful daughter, and went to the bottom of the stairs.

'Danny, I've got your shoes down here with your bag. Have you brushed your teeth?'

She heard the footsteps scampering across her bedroom on the way to the bathroom and sighed. Poor kid! The prospect of his first day at school was stressful enough without trying to get ready in a cottage that looked as if vandals had been let loose in it. Thank goodness he was the resilient sort.

The sound of running feet just seconds later told her that the tooth-brushing had been less than thorough, but there was no time to complain this morning. The last thing she wanted was for him to feel that she didn't have the time to see him properly settled for his first day at school before she went to work.

The sight of her precious son leaping down the narrow stairs two at a time was enough to have her heart in her throat, but it was marginally better than seeing him sliding down the precipitous banister rail. How was it that five-year-olds had absolutely no fear?

'Do you need any help?' she asked as he sat on the bottom step to tie his shoelaces, sorely tempted to snatch him up and wrap her arms around him for a hug. Where had the time gone? One minute he was a tiny helpless baby and the next he was old enough to be starting school. In some ways it hardly seemed any time at all since she'd attended the same school herself.

'Mum! I can do my laces myself, remember? I've been practising ready for school,' he reminded her proudly, his tongue stuck between his teeth as he concentrated on the task.

It was slower than if she'd done it for him, but it was another mark of his growing independence and she knew she shouldn't be tempted to smother him.

Even his hands reminded her of his father, already long-fingered and agile. Perhaps they, too, would be surgeon's hands. Strong and sensitive. Lover's hands…

'Mum…? I've been thinking.'

In spite of her momentary distraction, her mothering antennae vibrated at the change in tone of his voice.

'Thinking about what?' A quick glance at her watch confirmed that time was ticking away. Hopefully, this wouldn't be a major last-minute panic requiring a lot of reassurance. It wouldn't do for either of them to be late today of all days.

'Well, I know I'm big, now—big enough to go to *real* school—but I wondered…' He glanced up at her under thick dark lashes with a hint of uncertainty and she wanted to slay dragons for him. 'Can I still have a hug?'

'Oh, Danny, of course you can.' Her laughter was a little wobbly as she wrapped her arms around his sturdy little body. 'You can have as many hugs as you like for as many years as you like. You don't stop needing hugs just because you get older.'

'Even when I'm all grown up?' he asked in amazement, his deep blue eyes wide.

Tears threatened again when Sam realised that Danny apparently hadn't realised that adults liked hugs, too. Was it really that long since he'd seen it happen to her that he couldn't remember?

'If you're lucky, you'll still be having hugs even when you're a very old man…which could happen before we get you to school if we don't get moving. Now scoot!'

She swatted his little grey-trousered bottom and

grabbed her bag, then took a last despairing look round as she pulled the door closed and sighed. Wouldn't it be lovely if she could wave a magic wand and arrive back this afternoon to find everything tidily put away? Although where it was all going to go was a moot point. Danny's bedroom was about as big as a postage stamp. What she really needed was something about twice the size.

'Wishful thinking brings woeful want,' she murmured, then winced at the echo of one of her mother's favourite sayings.

Still, it was a sentiment that had got her through the last five and a half years with her emotions more or less intact. Unfortunately, moving so close to her mother might mean she had to practise some of her other maxims rather more frequently.

'Speech is silver but silence is golden,' she'd been reminded over the last twenty-eight years when she'd tried to voice an opinion, and 'Least said, soonest mended,' when discussions became heated.

But it was a fact of life that her mother was becoming older and, since her father had died, Sam couldn't in all conscience turn down the opportunity to work in the practice that served her home town. With the prospect of a hip replacement in the near future, the fact that they hadn't seen eye to eye for years didn't come into the equation.

Hopefully, the fact that her one and only grandson would now be living close enough to visit on a regular basis would engender some sort of family feeling. Five years was surely long enough for her to hold a grudge against an innocent child…

*   *   *

Sam sat in the car for a moment, blinking hard to hold back the emotional tears.

Danny had looked so little as he'd walked away from her, his hand trustingly held in his teacher's, that she'd been hard put not to cry. It wasn't as if he hadn't spent a great deal of his young life being cared for by other people. That was one of the disadvantages of being the child of a working mother.

He'd survived the hospital crèche and moved on to playgroup without any major traumas, but somehow, today was different. It was the first day of 'real' school and it seemed to mark a special milestone.

For the first time in a long time she permitted herself to wonder what his father would have said as he watched his son take that important step. Would he have been as proud as she was of his bravery and enthusiasm? Would he, too, have been just a little choked to realise just how fast their son was growing up?

With a determined shake of her head she reached forward to start the engine. So far this morning, in spite of the chaos surrounding them, she'd managed to keep to time. If she were to allow herself to look into that forbidden corner of her memory, the pain would probably cripple her. Was it Shakespeare who had said it was better to have loved and lost than never to have loved at all? Whoever it was had no idea how devastating it was to discover, first, that she was pregnant, and then, that the father of her child was dead, all in the space of a single day.

'Look on the bright side,' she could hear her mother saying, and was forced to agree that it was true. If she'd never known him and fallen in love with him, she wouldn't have her precious son, even though their startling resemblance was increasingly heartbreaking.

There was enough room in the car park behind the practice not to stretch her new driving skills. Owning her first car was exciting, but the fact that the ink on her licence was hardly dry was still rather nerve-racking.

It felt strange to realise that this flat area, half-surrounded by trees that had grown almost out of recognition in the last ten years, was almost the only feature remaining from the practice she'd known throughout her childhood.

Gone was the draughty old house with its inconvenient extensions and creaking wooden stairs.

In its place was a purpose-built unit, specially designed to cater for the needs of the new millennium.

Sam could only imagine the chaos that must have ensued when the pre-existing practice and cottage hospital buildings had been demolished to make way for the new combined facility, but could only admire the hardy souls who had had the vision to suggest it.

Built of local limestone, the Denison Memorial was an impressive building. It was traditional enough to fit comfortably with the cluster of buildings of nearby Edenthwaite, yet modern in its clean simplicity.

Sam had felt a shiver of awkwardness when she realised that her father's name had actually been incised into the stone above the main entrance. She realised that as a tribute to his lifetime of dedicated service to the community it was unparalleled, but to someone who had once answered to the same name there was a strangely creepy feel to it.

'Thank goodness old habits die hard,' she muttered as she pushed her door open and reached for her bag. 'The patients will probably still be calling it the Health Centre for the next twenty years.'

There was a nip to the spring air as she made her way to the door, the breeze flipping the edge of her jacket open and ruffling her hair. She ran her free hand through it, suddenly surprised to feel how short it was after so many years of wearing it long. For some reason, it had felt wrong to keep her 'crowning glory' when the whole of her world had been turned on its head, and she'd taken a pair of scissors to it. Was it just the fact that she'd come home that had made her forget?

These days it was more professionally shaped, when she had the time to make an appointment. As for her clothes... She pulled a rueful face. Thank goodness the generic smart suit was appropriate for both male and female GPs. This navy pinstripe teamed with various shirts and blouses was going to have to suffice for the foreseeable future—or at least until she found out what the dress code was around the practice.

'Good morning. Can I help you?' the receptionist said with a friendly smile, then did a double take. 'Sam? Is it really you? What are you doing here? Are you visiting your mother? She's not ill, is she? How long are you staying?'

'Hang on! Hang on!' Sam laughed. 'Let me answer one question before you ask the next dozen.'

'Well?' Paula Skillington demanded expectantly with her grin as broad as ever. Sam was certain that her old classmate would never change.

'Mother's fine, apart from her hip,' she began, si-

lently qualifying the pronouncement with the thought
that someone would have let her know if there *was*
anything amiss. She certainly wouldn't hear it from
the woman herself. 'And, no, I'm not here visiting
but to work.'

'Work? But…' Paula was uncharacteristically
speechless.

'Locum for Dr Potter,' Sam explained, taking pity
on her confusion.

'Oh, Lord, yes!' Paula was off and running again.
'I knew they were advertising for someone to take
over for her maternity leave, but with her having to
stop early it was going to be difficult. Most people
couldn't just drop everything at a moment's notice.'

No, most people couldn't, Sam agreed silently.
And she wouldn't have done so, either, if the fact
that she was still working with her ex-husband hadn't
become so uncomfortable. At least Andrew's position had allowed him to pull a few strings for her as
far as paperwork was concerned, which he had been
only too pleased to do if it meant she would be gone
all the sooner.

The rest had all been down to happy coincidence.
She'd only glanced through the adverts on the off
chance that there might be something suitable for a
part-time single mother and the name Edenthwaite
had jumped out at her.

Her phone call to her father's old partner, Norman
Castle, had brought her the astounding update that
high blood pressure had forced Grace Potter to stop
work early.

'My dear, if you want the job, it's yours,' Norman
had said bluntly.

'But don't you need me to fill in an application

form? Attend an interview?' she enquired weakly, stunned by the speed of events. 'Won't the others in the practice want to have a say in it?'

She'd only rung to make an initial enquiry, expecting to be told that they had more than enough applicants for such a plum job. Locum rates were considerably better than straight GP pay even though there was no continuity to the job. This sudden offer had taken her breath away and probably most of her brains if she was trying to talk him out of it. The fact that the job was for an initial six months was a bonus, too. It should allow her time to find another post within the area so she could stay close enough to her mother.

'In the ordinary way, you'd have to jump through all the usual hoops,' Norman confirmed dismissively. 'But we've known you since you were born and we've followed your career every step of the way. I don't suppose for a moment that there will be any problem confirming the appointment. We've got a good team here and none of us is in the business of cutting our nose off to spite our face. We can't do our best for our patients if there aren't enough of us to cope with the workload.'

Unable to believe her good luck, Sam had swiftly gathered enough breath to accept.

And here she was.

'Well, for better or worse, I'm the practice's new locum until Grace is ready to come back to work,' she confirmed for the delighted receptionist. 'At least, I will be if I don't get fired on the first day for loitering and gossiping!'

'Ouch!' Paula pulled a face. 'We'll have to catch up another time. You need to follow the signs to take you to the GP unit. It's on the ground floor of the West wing.'

Sam waved and took off in the right direction, reflecting briefly on the simplicity of the design of the new building.

She'd seen some of the first drawings when it was only at the planning stage and had noticed then that from the air it was shaped like a cross. The fact that each arm pointed to different points of the compass had made naming them simple.

'Even *I* shouldn't be able to get lost here,' she murmured, remembering the number of times she'd gone round in circles in the rabbit warrens that were some older hospitals.

That was how she and Daniel had first met, colliding as they turned a corner from opposite directions.

'I'm so sorry…' she'd blurted breathlessly, knowing she hadn't been watching where she was going in her hurry to find her way.

'Are you all right? Did I hurt you?' he'd demanded, holding her up by her arms when she would have fallen.

She'd looked up into deep blue eyes surrounded by the longest, thickest eyelashes she'd ever seen and her heart had performed a somersault. The fact that the rest of him was every bit as spectacular was too much to resist, especially when he smiled that sinfully wicked smile.

'Please say you're hurt,' he whispered huskily. He was leaning close enough for his breath to stir the strands of hair at her temple and she felt a shiver of response right down to her toes. 'Then I'd have an excuse to kiss it better.'

'Ah, there you are, my dear,' exclaimed a jovial voice and she returned to the present with a bump.

'Unc… Ah, Dr Castle.' She hoped that her voice sounded a little more steady than it felt. Why on earth was she letting her thoughts wander like this? There were more important things to do.

'Norman, my dear. Call me Norman, please,' he protested with a dismissive wave and a chuckle. 'We don't stand on ceremony when we're together in the practice. Anyway, now that we're both members of the same profession it would seem a little strange for you to continue calling me Uncle Norman.'

'I suppose it would,' she agreed and felt some of the tension begin to fade. This had been one of the things she had been worried about—the fact that her father had been the senior partner in the practice could have made for problems. She had been a frequent visitor throughout her childhood and it could have been difficult for those who had known her then to respond to her as an adult.

'Come on in and grab a cup of coffee. There's tea if you prefer. We've just got a couple of minutes before the onslaught starts so I thought I'd introduce you to the rest of the motley crew.'

Sam deposited her bag under the nearest seat and joined the older man at the coffee maker, taking a swift look around the room while she waited for her turn.

It was predictably bright and modern, but equally predictably bland as befitted a room where people had little interest in their surroundings other than as a place to relax for a few minutes. The best feature, in her opinion, was the tall pane of window that made up nearly half of the wall space, giving stupendous views of the surrounding countryside.

'We're not all here, of course,' he continued when he turned to hand her the cup he'd prepared to her specifications. 'There are seven of us GPs, full- and part-time—eight with you. You'll meet the others as the week goes on, but... Can I have your attention, people?' He raised his voice to include the other bodies scattered around the room. 'This is our new locum, Samantha Denison, come to take up the slack while Grace gets her feet up where they belong.'

There was a general murmur of greeting and Sam had to raise her voice a little to compete.

'Actually, it's Taylor, now,' she corrected, wishing she'd thought to remind him. The last thing she wanted was to put anyone's nose out of joint if they thought nepotism had got the job for her, rather than Norman's knowledge of her excellent results during her training. 'But the Sam is still the same.'

She'd actually considered taking back her maiden name when she and Andrew had divorced, but for Danny's sake had decided that it was easier if they both shared the same name.

'So, do I take it that Norman's known you for some time and is only now introducing us?' enquired a good-looking young man with sparkling green eyes.

'I've known her since before she was born, Jack,' Norman confirmed, smiling benignly as Sam shook hands with him. 'It's her father's name inscribed above the front door as you come in.'

'Oops! Should I be bowing and scraping?' he teased while his eyes flirted outrageously.

'Don't you dare, Jack...' She paused, waiting for him to fill in the blank.

'Jack Lawrence,' Norman supplied. 'He's also the son of a GP, so don't let him think he's fooling you with his pretence of awe.'

Jack pulled a resigned expression and Sam knew that, for all his testosterone-induced appraisal, she had probably found a new friend.

'And this is Frances Long,' Norman continued, gesturing towards the slightly harassed-looking woman flicking through a bulging diary as she perched on the arm of a chair.

'Frankie,' she corrected him quickly and looked up at Sam with a friendly grin. 'Delighted to have another woman on the team. With Grace ducking out, I was going to be the sole voice of sanity in this male-dominated wilderness!'

'Now, then, Frankie! Don't you encourage her to start ganging up on us. Our fragile male egos wouldn't be able to stand it,' Norman said with a mock frown. 'I hope you haven't been indoctrinating your girls with all that stuff?'

Frankie laughed but didn't deny the charge as Norman led Sam away.

'You probably won't remember me as I was the new boy here just before you went off to medical school. I'm Peter Caddick,' said a whip-thin gangling man as he held out his hand, the liveliness in his eyes belying the implications of his thinning greying hair. 'And as Frankie's two spend some of their time with my three, I can reassure you that they are turning out reasonably normal—for teenagers!'

Sam was chuckling now, delighted to find that there was such a good atmosphere between her new colleagues. It was such a relief to find that she was going to fit in so easily. In spite of her worries that she'd accepted the position without taking the time to consider all the implications, it looked as if the next six months were going to be a real pleasure.

'Ah! Here he is!' Norman said suddenly, gesturing over Sam's shoulder towards the door. 'Daniel, my boy. Come over here a minute. Sam, let me introduce you to the last member of our merry band on duty this morning. This good-looking young man is Daniel Hennessy.'

Sam turned with an easy smile on her face, looking forward to meeting yet another potential friend.

As if drawn by a powerful magnet her eyes fell immediately on the tall dark-haired man standing just inside the room and Norman's words seemed to echo into infinity through the roaring in her head.

She had an impression of heat as if something had splashed over her wrist and down onto her foot, and there was a distant sound as if china had shattered somewhere, but all she could see was a familiar pair of deep blue eyes.

She saw eyes like that every day when she looked at her son.

Daniel's eyes.

But this time they were in Daniel's face and that was impossible because Daniel had died more than five years ago.

CHAPTER TWO

'SAM! Look out!'

Norman's exclamation brought Sam out of her shock faster than her drenching with hot coffee.

Blinking, she looked down at the shattered fragments of cup lying at her feet and suddenly realised that her wrist and foot were stinging.

'Sit down, Sam,' ordered a deep voice and she didn't even have to look up to know that it was Daniel's, nor that it was his arm wrapped around her shoulder. The strange heated magnetism that had always flowed between the two of them was enough confirmation. 'Can somebody get a couple of wet towels to get the heat out of these scalds?' he asked, the question emerging more like a command.

Almost before she knew what was happening he'd guided her firmly into a chair and was kneeling at her feet to remove her shoe.

'Tights or stockings?' he demanded gruffly as he took her foot in his hand but all she could do was stare at him wordlessly.

She'd loved this man with all her heart and soul and for over five years she had mourned his death. Even bearing his son had done little to assuage her grief. The fact that she'd been unable to forget Daniel had been the basic reason for the failure of her relationship with Andrew.

So how was it possible that he was alive, here, in front of her?

Was she trapped in some dreadful nightmare? Would she wake up in a moment and discover that her move to Edenthwaite was nothing more than a figment of her imagination?

'Speak to me, Sam! Are you wearing tights or stockings?' Daniel demanded harshly, his hand tightening briefly around her ankle. 'We need to get them off or you're going to blister. They're holding the heat against your skin.'

'Th-they're sort of like long socks,' she stammered, still lost in a daze and watched wide-eyed as he briskly slid her trouser leg up to her knee and stripped the nylon off her foot.

There was a weird sensation of déjà vu as she looked down on his dark head. He'd done something similar for her the day a passing car had sent a puddle cascading over her feet. *That* time, he hadn't stopped at removing her stockings and shoes. His hands had been warm but he'd insisted that she needed a shower to thaw out her freezing feet. It had been almost inevitable that they would end up sharing the shower.

'Does that feel easier?' he asked, dragging her out of her bittersweet memories to the realisation that both her wrist and foot were now swathed in cold wet towels.

'Oh, my dear, I'm so sorry,' Norman interrupted, clearly stricken with remorse. 'I must have knocked the cup right out of your hand. How could I have been so clumsy?'

'Oh, Norman, no!' she exclaimed, reaching out with her good hand to clasp his. 'It *wasn't* your fault. I…I lost my grip on it, that's all. And anyway,' she added hurriedly when he still looked doubtful, 'it wasn't as if the coffee was really hot. I'd already been holding it for several minutes while you made the introductions. It…it was the shock, more than anything.' Her father's old partner wasn't to know which shock she was talking about—the dousing with coffee or the shock of seeing Daniel standing there.

Norman was finally mollified, but she could tell from her fleeting glance at Daniel that he had recognised the ambiguity in her words.

'Actually, it was probably my fault as much as anyone's,' he announced as he straightened up to his full height and loomed almost menacingly over her…or was that her over-active imagination taking over? 'Sam was probably surprised to meet me again. We haven't seen each other for…what is it, Sam? Five years or more? Quite a surprise, obviously.'

There was a chorus of delight at the unexpected coincidence and her new colleagues were clearly interested in details but Daniel was obviously not interested in satisfying them.

Since he'd taken care of her injuries he seemed to have withdrawn into himself, almost as if he wanted nothing further to do with her.

She couldn't help the way her eyes clung to him and she wanted nothing more than that everyone should disappear and leave the two of them together to talk. He obviously didn't feel the same way as, with a last wordless glower in her direction he silently turned and walked away, only pausing to take a small stack of letters out of the pigeonhole marked with his name and pick up his bag.

Without another word or even so much as a glance

over his shoulder he left the room, the door swinging
slowly closed behind him.

'Well, there's a thing,' Frankie murmured into the
lingering silence, speculation in her tone. 'For the
last three years that man has been composure itself,
and the day you arrive...' She glanced at Sam with
a quizzical eyebrow raised but to her relief didn't
take the thought any further.

It was embarrassing enough that such a scene
should have happened within the first few minutes of
meeting her new colleagues, but her loss of composure barely registered when set against the disturbing
discovery she'd made. It had only been a glance and
a fleeting one at that, but she couldn't forget the totally unexpected animosity she'd glimpsed in
Daniel's expression.

Over the hubbub of renewed conversation around
her there was a swift tap on the door and a young
female face appeared in the gap.

'I have the start of an impatient horde building up
in the waiting room,' she announced cheerfully. 'If
we don't want the whole system to grind to a halt,
it would probably be a good idea if you all...'

'All right, Jane! All right,' Peter Caddick interrupted good-naturedly. 'Such a shame for one so
young to be such a dreadful slave-driver. Sam, meet
Jane Pelly, the youngest of the three dragons who
guard our gate and wield the whip. And don't think
that just because you're a woman that she'll treat you
differently. She's an equal-opportunities bully.'

Jane's laugh as she withdrew her head was evidence that this was an ongoing taunt, but somehow
this further proof of the good relationships within the

practice failed to register properly. Nothing seemed to be making much sense at the moment.

Everything came down to one astounding discovery and all Sam could think about was the fact that Daniel wasn't dead.

Furthermore, for some totally inexplicable reason, he seemed to be deeply angry with her.

Sam had never been so grateful for nothing to do and plenty of time to do it.

In spite of her determination to start work immediately, Norman had decided that her first day would be taken up with orientation rather than taking a surgery for their incapacitated colleague.

'There are no special clinics today, so it's a relatively light load. Tomorrow will be soon enough to climb into harness,' he'd said firmly. 'First, let me show you around our pride and joy. You probably remember that it was your father who did most of the lobbying for the combined hospital and health centre. I'll never forget the day we finally got the go-ahead…'

Time sped by and when she next glanced at her watch from the comfort of one of the chairs in the staff lounge above the GP surgery wing, she was amazed to realise that it was lunch-time already. As she was only just beginning to feel as if her brain was functioning properly it was probably a very good thing she hadn't been responsible for anyone's health this morning.

As she'd expected, there hadn't been any real damage from her accident with the cup of coffee. The skin of her wrist and foot had been red for a while but Daniel's swift response with the cold wet towels had meant that within an hour there was only a little residual tenderness.

Her bewilderment over Daniel's antagonism was far longer lasting and had gradually given way to anger of her own.

She had loved the man, dammit, and had believed him when he said that he loved her, too. She had also believed him when he said that he'd had to go away to deal with a family emergency, and believed that he was going to contact her as soon as he reached his destination.

A week without word had turned concern into worry until she'd finally used the number he'd given her in case of emergencies.

'I'm sorry, miss,' said a strongly accented voice on the other end of the line half a world away. Whoever it was sounded old and frail and was clearly upset. 'Doctor Hen'sy can not come to the telephone no more. Doctor Hen'sy, he dead. Killed dead by the bad mens.'

Sam didn't remember how she'd ended the conversation. It was some time later that she realised she was still holding the receiver while a mechanical voice urged her to please hang up and try again.

For several days her world had been filled with disbelief and denial. It was impossible. How *could* Daniel be dead when she loved him and was carrying his child?

The final straw had been the painfully brief hand-written letter she'd received from Colin and Joyce Hennessy inviting her to join the family at the funeral of their son.

Daniel had never spoken much about his family.

The fact that he had clearly spoken to his parents about her had finally breached the dam that had built up inside her. For the first time since she'd heard the news she began to sob, shedding deep soul-wrenching tears that didn't really stop until several days later.

Afterwards, she would look back on that time and marvel at the fact that she hadn't lost her precious baby. His continuing presence inside her was the only thing that had made sense in a world gone mad. He was the one thing that seemed to make life worth living; something to hang on to; a part of Daniel's genetic inheritance that would still exist even though he did not. He was her own private salvation.

Not that her mother had agreed when Sam came home to tell them about her situation.

The less she remembered about that disastrous scene the better, Sam thought with a grimace. As far as her parents had been concerned, she was letting them down, compromising the family name with an illegitimate child. Her mother had even blamed her for precipitating her father's stroke.

It was probably her desire to try to make amends that had prompted her to leap into her disastrous marriage to Andrew.

They'd known each other since they started their training together but it wasn't until he found her breaking her heart after her dreadful meeting with her parents that she confided in him and he ventured his proposal.

Unfortunately, they found that the road to hell really *was* paved with good intentions and realised all too soon that they'd made a mistake.

It didn't matter how hard Sam tried to forget

Daniel, or Andrew tried to believe that he could accept another man's child as his own, by the time Danny arrived they each knew that the arrangement was doomed.

At least the legitimacy of it had mollified her parents at the time, but the strain of pretence wasn't worth the effort when it was making both of them unhappy. Finally, she and Andrew had admitted failure and set about quietly rectifying the situation.

The two of them were far happier now that they were nothing more than distant friends, but Sam only had to think about her mother's reaction to her recent divorce to know that she was unlikely ever to have a close mother-and-daughter relationship with her.

When she let herself think about it, Sam had always believed that everything would have been so different if Daniel had lived; if she and Daniel had married. Today's revelation had violently derailed those thoughts from their usual 'if only' track.

'Why did he do it? Why did *they* do it?' she murmured in a voice made tight with pain and disbelief, startling herself with the realisation that she'd spoken the words aloud. She bit her lips and hurried for the seclusion of the staff washroom, trying to keep the rest of her thoughts inside.

Even then, she found herself whispering, needing to hear her wildly whirling ideas out loud to make them real.

'If he didn't want to see me any more, all he had to do was tell me,' she said as she fought back tears, uneasy with the newly desolate expression confronting her in the mirror. 'They didn't have to set up some sort of family conspiracy to get rid of me.'

She stood still and silent for a moment as the last

sentence played around and around in her head, each repetition sounding more and more ludicrous.

No rational adult would go to the length of staging a funeral to help a son shake off an unwanted girl-friend. Certainly none outside of a work of crazed fiction, and especially not the sort of warm, caring people Daniel had described when he'd spoken of his parents.

Then there was his reaction to seeing her today. He'd been surprised, yes, but this had been so much more than the response of a man meeting up with an old girlfriend.

Something wasn't right, and the sooner she tracked the man down and asked him point blank why he *had* disappeared from her life without a word, the better.

Frankie had already noticed the uncomfortable atmosphere between the two of them when they'd met face to face today.

Sam had agreed to filling the part-time locum post for an initial six months while Grace was on mater-nity leave, but she was actually hoping that she might be asked to stay on as a permanent member of staff once Grace was ready to return.

She realised that she was never going to be able to work with Daniel without spoiling the happy tone if they didn't get things sorted out.

She had come home! Samantha Denison…no, make that Samantha Taylor. She was married, now, and had come back to her home town when she'd always vowed it was the one thing she would never do!

Daniel sat numbly behind the desk in his room and

stared blindly out of the window while he grappled with the situation.

Ordinarily, the view of the stark Cumbrian hills girdled by the last of the springtime necklaces of blossoming hawthorn would have delighted him. All he could see now was his mental image of the woman he'd once loved with all his heart and soul.

She'd changed.

Gone was the laughing girl/woman he remembered with her dark brown hair shimmering with coppery highlights almost to her waist. Her grey-blue eyes were different, too, and not just because they were framed with a new short gamine hairstyle. Once those eyes had been filled with life, glimmering almost like sunlight on the surface of one of the nearby lakes. They were more sombre, now, with a harder, almost metallic sheen as though shadowed by some painful event she'd gone through during the years since he'd last seen her.

He shook his head, trying to dispel the sympathy that began to well up.

He was far too soft-hearted.

When he'd realised who was standing there in front of him he'd been stunned into immobility with a surge of the same desire that had always assailed him when he'd seen her. He'd been relieved when it was briefly suppressed by a searing flash of the anger that had helped him to cope with five years of bitter memories, but then she'd spilt her coffee and all he was conscious of was concern.

'Too soft-hearted,' he repeated. 'She was surrounded by people, but who was the first one at her side checking to see how badly she'd been injured? Who was the one ordering wet towels to wrap around her reddened wrist and ankle while he sat her down in a chair as gently as if she were Dresden china?' He gave an exasperated snort.

When would he ever learn that she didn't need his sympathy? She didn't need him at all and obviously never had, in spite of her protestations of love. There was always going to be someone else for her to turn to and with Jamie to take care of he didn't need that sort of disruption in his life. It didn't matter that she was the woman who had once made him feel willing to slay dragons.

'Slay dragons? Ha!' he scoffed aloud, but was uncomfortably aware that the feeling hadn't gone away even after five years. He'd actually been tempted to indulge in a ridiculous testosterone-induced display when he'd seen the blatant appreciation of her in Jack Lawrence's eyes.

'Enough is enough,' he declared firmly, straightening up out of his chair and reaching for his bag. 'She might be working here for the next few months, but that's all there is to it.' After all this time he should be accustomed to the idea that she was permanently out of his life. She'd made her choice and he'd had to get on with his life without her, even if the mere sight of her still set his pulse racing.

'Self-control, that's all I need.'

He threw a last glance out of the window in search of the calm he would need to deal with the rest of the day.

A cloud crossing the sun cast a shadow over the slope of the nearest hill to give it a brooding air and he had to consciously shrug off the feeling that it was somehow symbolic.

He and Jamie were happy together. They had his

mother nearby, widowed now and all too willing to spend the night babysitting when it was Daniel's turn on call. Why would he even dream of letting a fickle woman back into his life to mess everything up?

He gave a decisive nod, glad to have got his scattered thoughts in order at last. Unfortunately, mere logic didn't stop the ache. It had wrapped itself around his heart in the breath-stealing moment that he'd first recognised that unforgettable pair of blue-grey eyes.

He was avoiding her! He must be, otherwise she'd have seen him at some stage during the day. She'd seen all the others at least once and seemed to have bumped into Jack Lawrence almost every five minutes.

Her dejected mood couldn't help but lighten when she thought about that man. He was an impossible flirt but she was sure that there was absolutely no malice in the man. Perhaps, when she had sorted things out with Daniel, there might be a chance that a friendship could develop between herself and Jack…maybe even something deeper…

She contemplated the idea for a moment then shook her head. With Daniel on the same staff, there was little likelihood that her stupid heart would even let her notice another man, let alone fall in love with him.

Paula could probably tell her where Daniel was, but the last thing Sam wanted to do was ask questions about his whereabouts. She knew how quickly rumours could get started in a community as small as a hospital, and most of the people in this one had known her since she was born. All she could do for now was keep an eye out for him and pin him down for a long-overdue explanation.

In the meantime, she was pretty certain that even if she couldn't manage it blindfolded, she would at least be able to find her way around Denison Memorial without getting lost.

It was quite easy, once she'd got the hang of it. The North wing housed four four-bedded wards on the ground floor, two of which comprised a specially equipped geriatric unit while the others were for general use.

Above was the miniature maternity department— a four-bedded Domino unit and two single rooms with a well-equipped delivery suite.

'I'm really looking forward to delivering my first baby in there,' she'd exclaimed as she ran an approving eye over the compact design and up-to-date equipment.

'You could strike lucky sooner than you think,' Norman had warned her with a twinkle in his eye as he led her on to the next stop. 'There are several mums getting ready to pop during the next few weeks. I'll have to see if I can arrange for them to deliver during your on-call nights!'

The ground floor of the West wing was reserved for casualties and day clinics such as the fortnightly visit from an orthopaedic specialist. It had direct access from the ambulance bay outside and boasted a separate restroom and control centre for the paramedics and drivers.

'That doesn't stop them from coming up and joining the rest of us,' Norman pointed out. 'Especially when they've finished all their biscuits. Actually,' he continued thoughtfully, 'we've been very lucky with staff here. Right from the first, there's been a good atmosphere. It sounds corny, but it's almost like a family, the way everyone works together. Not that we don't have some pretty stormy staff meetings when someone's putting forward a pet project! But on a personal level...'

His glowing words made her more determined than ever that she and Daniel should settle their differences. There was no way she wanted to be the cause of an unhappy element. All she needed was a few minutes. How long could it take for him to tell her why his parents had invited her to his funeral when he was plainly still in the land of the living?

Norman proudly shouldered open the next set of doors and she found herself facing a small but perfectly adequate theatre.

'When it was designed, it was only intended to cope with the sort of minor surgeries that a GP could reasonably be expected to tackle. Of course, having Daniel on hand has changed that a bit,' he admitted with a conspiratorial grin. 'Once the smaller GP practices found out about his surgical skills they actually started directing some of their accident patients here rather than sending them on the much longer trip into the big city hospital.'

The idea that Daniel's surgical skills were sought after filled her with silent pride but that didn't stop her seeing the pitfalls.

'Is that fair on him?' she asked quietly, not stopping to think how her instinctive defence of the man would strike her father's old friend. 'It puts an awful lot of responsibility on one pair of shoulders, especially when he's only working with the basics.'

Norman chuckled. 'If you want to talk about working with the basics, you should talk to the man. This set-up is positively luxurious in comparison with the last place he worked.'

Sam was startled by his implication.

Once she'd accepted the fact that Daniel hadn't died she'd automatically assumed that he had continued with his intention of becoming a GP. After all, that was where he had ended up.

Now Norman was hinting that his journey to Denison Memorial hadn't been such a straight route after all and she discovered she'd been given more food for thought. There was obviously more than one secret in Daniel's past, a fact that made her rather distracted during the rest of her orientation tour.

She'd already seen part of the South wing ground floor, a large part of it being taken up with the main reception area. There was also a pharmacy used not only for dispensing drugs to patients within the hospital but also those who travelled in to see a doctor from the large number of outlying villages, hamlets and farms.

Above the main reception was the department devoted to administration and hospital records. They did little more than stick their noses round the door, but it was enough for Sam to see that the whole area was bristling with the latest in state-of-the-art computers. 'Thank goodness, there's still got a long way to go before we completely replace manila envelopes full of paper records with computer files,' Norman said with a grimace. 'We've all gone on a course so that we can handle the computers, but I doubt that most of us old-timers will ever be completely comfortable with it. Your father was the same. He always said that it wasn't the same as being able to get your hands on a piece of paper and read it.'

'And yet he was always insistent on staying ab-solutely up to date with medical matters,' Sam pointed out with her tongue firmly in her cheek. 'And they say women are hard to understand!'

By now, the two of them had returned to the cen-tral hub from which each arm of the building branched. This time she was able to take a moment to notice that it boasted a collection of plants that obviously thrived in the natural light pouring down from the large skylight right up in the roof.

There was a scattered group of more comfortable chairs here and volunteers manned a little coffee shop where they also sold snacks and home-made cakes. It was clear that the little oasis was very pop-ular with visitors and the more ambulant patients, and Sam wondered how long it would be before she found the time to sit down and relax.

'Obviously not today,' she murmured to herself as Norman set off down the fourth arm of the building and she hurried to follow.

This was the East wing of the cross and would be where she spent the majority of her time from to-morrow onwards.

The ground floor housed the GP practice. There were eight rooms in all, each compact and functional and none of them in any way luxurious. There was a separate special little domain for the practice nurse and a small team of receptionists whose job it was to keep each doctor's list running smoothly.

'So, my dear, what do you think of us?' Norman demanded as he perched himself on the edge of the examination couch in the corner of the room that was to be hers. 'Do you think you'll be happy working here?'

'I think it's wonderful,' Sam said wholeheartedly. 'I can vaguely remember when the whole project was first being talked about. You and Dad had all those drawings spread out over the dining room table on more than one occasion.' She'd actually sneaked in and had a closer look when no one was looking, impressed, but knowing that this wasn't the sort of hospital she would one day work in. It would never be large enough for the paediatrics department she envisaged in her future.

But then, here she was, her future having taken off in a completely different direction.

'It's just amazing to see the drawings come to life like this,' she finished with a smile, knowing that her regrets for the paediatrics career she'd had to abandon was more than made up for by her precious son.

'It is, certainly, but what I meant was, do you think you'll be happy working here?' he probed. 'It's a far cry from the big city hospitals you're used to.'

'And thank goodness for that,' she retorted. 'I'd far rather bring my son up in Edenthwaite than in some of the places we've lived.'

'Ah!' He pounced. 'So there's a chance you might be thinking about settling?'

A swarm of thought and answers collided inside her head, each fighting for supremacy.

Yes, she would like to stay in the area for Danny's sake and so that she could be there for her mother. Yes, she would like the chance to work in such pleasant surroundings and in such a well-equipped and apparently well-run facility. But, there was no way she could contemplate committing herself to working here on a permanent basis until she'd sorted out a few things in her private life.

'At the moment, I'm taking it one day at a time,' she said evasively. 'I haven't even had a chance to unpack my suitcases, yet, so let's wait and see what the next six months bring.'

CHAPTER THREE

THE knock on her door came just as Sam collapsed into her chair and reached out for her celebratory glass of red wine.

'Who on earth is that?' she grumbled as she heaved herself to her bare feet and padded out of the minuscule lounge towards the front door.

Danny had been even more reluctant to go to bed than usual because he'd had so much to tell her about his first day at school.

Everything had been recounted in the minutest detail, including the fact that there was another boy in his class called Daniel James.

'But everyone calls him Jamie instead of Danny, so we won't get muddled up,' her little son announced proudly.

Finally, his batteries had run down enough for her to get him to put his head on his pillow, and he'd gone out like a light.

Since then, she'd spent all evening getting the place straight and felt she'd earned her little self-indulgent reward. Whoever it was outside her cottage was going to have to excuse her being less than perfectly welcoming in her grubby old clothes. All she'd wanted was a few minutes of relaxation before she had a shower and went to her own bed.

She was already formulating a polite apology as she switched on the porch light and swung the door open.

The words froze to her tongue when she saw the figure caught in the yellow lamplight.

'Daniel,' she breathed as her heart gave several extra beats before settling into a heavier rhythm.

'Sam,' he said quietly, his eyes so darkly intent that they almost seemed black as he took in the ratty old jeans and paint-splattered shirt she'd changed into after her orientation day. 'May I come in? I thought we ought to talk before you start work. Clear the air?'

She'd been wanting to speak to him all day but, now that he was here, all she wanted to do was shut the door.

It would have been different if they'd arranged to meet somewhere. She'd have had time to prepare herself. She certainly wouldn't be looking like something the cat dragged in.

Coward! she castigated herself as she took a step back and silently pulled the door wide.

She would rather this wasn't taking place in her home, she thought as she gestured for him to enter. Now she would be able to picture the way his lean height seemed to dominate the small cosy confines of the little room and the way his broad shoulders and long legs dwarfed the cottage-style furniture when he took the chair she indicated.

The trouble was, he looked as if he actually belonged here in her new home, and that couldn't be right.

'Can I get you anything? Tea? Coffee?' Unless he'd changed a great deal since she'd first met him, there was no point offering him a glass of her celebratory wine. He made a point of avoiding alcohol completely if he was going to be driving.

'Nothing, thanks.' He gave his head a single shake

and she was startled to see the lamplight gleam on the start of grey in his dark hair.

Daniel was going grey already? He was only in his early thirties. Thirty-two? At least it seemed as thick and healthy as ever. It would have been unfair if he had been going bald, too.

'So...' She tried to get her brain in order. What business was it of hers if he'd lost all of his hair or gone completely white? The fact that the few silver strands looked good on him was none of her business, either.

'Are you going to hover there or will you be sitting down? This could take more than a couple of minutes,' he suggested quietly with a pointed glance. She felt the warmth of a blush envelop her as she sank back into her own chair and she hurried to retrieve her glass from the nearby table. Perhaps she could hide behind it for a moment. Perhaps he would think the flustered colour in her face was a reflection from the wine.

'I take it you didn't know I was working here...in Edenthwaite,' he said, the words more statement than question.

'Any more than you knew I was joining the practice,' she countered.

He nodded again in acknowledgement. 'I was away for a few days so didn't know anything about Grace's problem until I walked in this morning. Norman explained that he'd had to find a replacement for her in a hurry and none of the locums who were available for her official maternity leave could come so quickly. He said that you'd fallen into his lap like a ripe plum.'

'Just a case of being in the right place at the right

time,' she said dismissively while silently relishing the implied compliment. 'My mother is due to go in for her hip replacement soon so I was looking for something within reasonable travelling distance. This post couldn't be better because it means that I'll be close enough to keep an eye on her without it seeming too obvious—at least until she's properly on her feet again.'

She waited for the next question but it didn't come, and the silence started to stretch out uncomfortably.

From her chair she had a clear view of his face silhouetted against the buttery yellow light. Even after more than five years it was still so familiar that a tight fist seemed to close around her heart.

She wasn't still in love with him. She couldn't be in love with someone who would deliberately hurt her the way he had.

All those days of recognising him in every dark-haired man, all those nights of waking up with tears in her eyes as she relived their happy times.

She'd loved him and he'd said he loved her, so what had gone wrong?

'Why did you pretend you were dead?' she demanded suddenly, unable to bear the suspense any longer. Her voice was unexpectedly loud in the quiet room but that wouldn't account for the shocked expression on his face.

'Dead?' he repeated, clearly astonished. 'Who said I was dead? When?'

'Everyone,' she said with a jerky gesture. 'First, the woman when I tried to phone you, then your mother...'

'My *mother* said I was dead?' he echoed blankly.
'When?'

'When she sent me the letter inviting me to your funeral,' she said, the feeling of horror reverberating through her memories all over again.

'Oh, God,' he groaned and closed his eyes, his head dropping back against the back of the chair. 'It wasn't *my* funeral. It was my brother's.'

'Your brother? But...' There was so much she hadn't known about him...still didn't know. She'd never even realised he had a brother. 'But, when I phoned... The woman I spoke to... I specifically asked to speak to Dr Hennessy and she said you were dead; that the bad men had killed you.'

'James, my brother, was a doctor, too,' he said quietly, his voice rough. 'He was heavily into voluntary medical work in what used to be called third world countries. He'd been doing another stint with an emergency medical relief team in an area that should have been neutral when things started to get dangerous. He phoned me to come and get Maggie out.'

'Maggie?'

'His wife,' he supplied briefly. 'She was a nurse, equally dedicated and working with the same outfit. They met on a previous mission and married a few months later.'

'She *was*...?' Sam had picked up on the telltale word. 'She died, too?'

He nodded. 'If there'd been any way I could have arrived twenty-four hours earlier...but the only way into the region was to travel out with the next shipment of humanitarian aid.'

'What happened?' she prompted gently. Even in

the subdued lighting it was clear from his expression that he was reliving the trauma.

'A group of local "freedom fighters" decided that they were going to hijack the food and medicine and sell them to the highest bidders. That way they could get the money to finance their political aims.'

Sam could remember all too clearly the atrocities that had been spread over the national news. Her own grief had been so intense that she hadn't been able to bear it and had stopped watching the television entirely.

'James was equally determined that the supplies should be used for his patients, so they went on a rampage through the makeshift hospital and killed him.'

'Oh, Daniel.' Everything in her cried out to offer comfort; to wrap her arms around him until the devastation eased.

Gradually, the details of what he'd told her sank in. She felt the same compassion for his family in the loss of James as she had when she'd believed it was Daniel who had died, but this time there was another element.

For all this time she'd had to try to come to terms with the fact that he was never coming back. Now she realised that there was one last question.

'Daniel, why didn't you come back?' she asked in a voice that quivered. 'You knew I was waiting.'

As if her words were the final straw he leapt to his feet and towered over her, his eyes shooting daggers that pinned her into her seat.

'Ah, but I did, and you weren't,' he said rawly. 'I came back and you *weren't* waiting.'

She shook her head, desperately wanting to argue,

to explain, but in the face of his clear anger, she couldn't find the words.

She'd held on to a thin thread of hope that the elderly woman she'd spoken to on the telephone had made a mistake, right up until Mrs Hennessy had invited her to the funeral. After that, nothing had mattered to her any more except carrying Daniel's child and providing a secure future for him.

'Three weeks,' he ground out, his hands clenched into tight fists around the wooden arms of the chair. 'I came back as soon as I could and found you'd got married three weeks after I left.'

'Doctor, will you have time to see another patient before you go out on your visits?' Sam recognised the voice of the GP unit's most senior receptionist, Anne Townsend, on the telephone. 'Only I've got a Mrs Janet Ashland here and she's in a bit of a state.'

Sam glanced across at the curtained corner of the room where her last patient was dressing again, glad that the old system of intercom had been updated to the greater privacy of a telephone, then glanced at her wrist. It seemed that everything was going to be a juggling act if she was going to be free to collect Danny from school each day. It wouldn't be so bad if she were a more confident driver. As it was, she was afraid that her home visits were going to take a long time.

'Is she on Grace's list? Have we got any notes?'

'She used to go to your father but she's one of Jack's, now. He hasn't got a surgery until tomorrow morning, but frankly I don't think she can wait.'

'OK. Give me a couple of minutes then send her in,' she agreed, mentally deciding that she might have to eat her sandwiches 'on the run' today if she was going to be back in time. It wouldn't do anything for her digestion but perhaps she'd finally lose those extra pounds she'd never been able to shift since Danny was born.

'Mrs Ashland? Do take a seat.' She could see what Anne Townsend meant, Sam thought as the heavily pregnant woman lowered herself onto the chair. Her face was quite grey and pinched and looked far older than the age on her file. 'Now, how can I help you?'

The young woman worried at her lip for a moment before she drew in a shuddering breath. 'I don't think you can,' she said at last, tears glimmering. 'I don't think anyone can.'

Sam drew in a breath of her own and sent a prayer upwards that she'd find the right approach. There was obviously something serious going on here.

'Will you tell me about it, anyway?' she offered with an encouraging smile and waited. One missed lunch wouldn't matter much in the scheme of things, after all.

'It's Mark. My husband,' she whispered, finally, the words starting as a trickle and escalating rapidly to a flood. 'I'm so afraid he's going to do something...something drastic.' A lone tear trickled down her cheek but she didn't even seem to notice. 'Ever since the accident he's been getting more and more depressed and with the baby due so soon... I can't be watching him all the time, see?'

'What sort of accident did he have? A car crash?' Sam prompted, trying to focus the poor woman's mind on questions and answers rather than her overloaded emotions.

'No. It was on the farm. He'd been trying his hand

at coppicing some willows down the boggy end of the farm. The wood can be turned into charcoal for barbecues and the whippy lengths for art and suchlike. These days it's not enough to rear animals to earn a living. He'd been using the shredder to get rid of the scrub when it jammed. When he tried to clear it, he got his hand trapped. It was so badly damaged that they had to take it off.'

The stark simplicity of the narrative made Sam wince, then hope her patient hadn't noticed her reaction.

'Right or left?' As if that made much difference when the man was possibly suicidal.

'Right. And he's always been very right-handed. But that isn't the worst of it. He says he can still feel the hand, as if it's still there. See, it's the pain that's driving him mad. If he could only sleep at night then I could sleep, too. Could you give him some tablets to knock him out, perhaps?'

Sam had put the box of tissues within reach and she used the time while a handful were used to mop up to go over what she'd been told.

It sounded as if the poor man was suffering from something called phantom limb pain. She hadn't actually come across it before, other than in her studies, but knew that it was a neuropathic condition in which the brain continued to send out and receive signals as if a missing limb were still there.

'Mrs Ashland, I can't prescribe tablets for your husband without seeing him. Do you think you could persuade him to make an appointment to come in? It doesn't necessarily have to be with me, if he'd feel more comfortable seeing one of the other doctors.'

'Will they give him some tablets? Only I don't

know how long I can go on like this. And the baby's due so soon.'

'Is he looking forward to the baby coming?' Sam asked, trying to eliminate the possibility that there were other reasons why the poor man was in such a desperate state.

'He was over the moon about it...until the accident,' she said sadly. 'Even made a little crib for it, with rockers on, too. And decorated the bedroom. He was even counting off the days on the calendar, but not any more. Now all he can think about, when he's not actually pushing himself to work, is the dreadful pain he can feel in a hand that's not even there.'

Deep in her memory something was stirring, but it wasn't clear enough for Sam to grasp. This wasn't the time or the place for her to stare off into the distance, either.

'He's still managing to work?'

'Oh, yes! Harder than ever!' Janet exclaimed with a weary smile for Sam's obvious ignorance. 'Farm work doesn't go away just because you've had an accident or you're waiting for a baby to arrive. We can't afford to pay a man to do the work even though everything takes so much longer, now. Anyway, he says the only time he can switch off to the pain a bit is if he's really grafting at something.'

Sam could only imagine how hard the man was having to work to manage the amount of work he formerly accomplished with two hands. And it wasn't as if his wife could lend much of a hand at present.

It was difficult to know what to say. There certainly wasn't a magic wand she could wave to solve the problem.

'At the moment, all I can suggest is that you talk to him and try to get him to talk to you. Men being what they are, he's probably hiding the fact that he's worried about your reaction to his injuries. Perhaps he feels ugly, now. Perhaps he feels he's failed you, especially with the baby due any day. Perhaps he just feels as if he's lost control of everything, and with the pain on top of that…'

'You mean, it could just be the last straw that breaks the camel's back?' Janet's hand was closed tightly around the wad of soggy tissues, but she was clearly an intelligent woman and Sam could see that her suggestions had set her thinking.

'It's a possibility,' she suggested. 'Just by coming in to talk to me, I know you care for him, but you've got to make sure *he* knows it, too. Make sure that he knows you love him, you're worried about him and want to help him—and try to persuade him to come in. In the meantime, I'm going to get in contact with the surgeon who did the operation, and do some research of my own to see if I can find out anything that would help. Even if it's only to get the name of the best tablets for him.

'In the meantime, make sure you keep talking to him. Don't let him go off brooding, even if it means you have to ask him to help you in the house. I'm sure you could find something that needs moving, or even a backache that needs a bit of a massage,' she added with a sly grin.

There was a more positive angle to the slender shoulders as the young woman bade her goodbye and Sam mentally crossed her fingers that young Mr Ashland wouldn't be driven to do anything drastic before they could find a way to help him.

She groaned when she caught sight of the time and scooped up the pile of patient files with one hand and her jacket and bag with the other.

No time for any sort of lunch today if she was going to be on time to pick Danny up from school, and if she got lost on one of her home visits...

'Oh, Dr Hennessy,' she heard Anne Townsend call after her dark-haired nemesis as he entered the reception area. Sam silently cursed the way her pulse skipped. If she didn't stop reacting to his name this way she was going to end up a nervous wreck. 'There was a phone call for you while you were in with your last patient. Mrs Hennessy rang. Could you ring her back, please?'

Sam felt as if time froze around her.

Mrs Hennessy rang...echoed endlessly inside her head as she gazed at those familiar deep blue eyes in that lean, clever face.

Oh, God, he was married.

The realisation reverberated through her with the force of a mortal blow.

Why had she never considered that he might be married?

Granted, she hadn't had long to get used to the idea that he was alive, but for some strange reason, she'd almost presumed that he would still be the same man he was when they'd been together.

Had she actually been harbouring secret thoughts about the possibility that they might take up where they'd left off five years ago? Stupid woman! As if his life would have stood still like that.

For all his apparent anger when he'd visited her cottage, he'd revealed that he'd known about her marriage all along. Evidently he'd dealt with it quite

easily five years ago and gone on with his life without a qualm.

So much for the love she'd believed they'd shared,
she thought angrily as she slid behind the wheel to
begin her trek around the district. Obviously it had
all been one-sided.

Yes, she'd married Andrew, but she'd never have
considered it if she'd thought Daniel was alive.
Andrew had held out a lifeline and she had been too
devastated and confused to see what a disaster it
would be for them both.

The road outside the school was lined almost end-to-
end with parked cars as parents waited for their dar-
lings to emerge. Just one space remained, but Sam
certainly didn't have enough courage to manoeuvre
her vehicle into it with a critical audience looking
on.

It wouldn't be so bad if it were just women con-
gregating for a chat by the gates. They would have
had some sympathy for her if she didn't manage it
first time. The sight of several men in the group sent
her right to the end of the queue, well out of sight.
It might mean a longer walk, but what did that matter? She could do with the exercise after nearly three
hours of driving over hills and down dales in search
of elusive addresses.

She'd barely had time to do more than exchange
a couple of smiles when she heard the sound of the
bell.

Almost instantly a horde of children exploded into
the playground with coats and bags flying as they ran
towards their waiting parents.

The first time Sam had seen it happen she'd wondered how the smallest children didn't get flattened in the rush, then she'd realised that they were actually the ones who were running fastest and shouting loudest.

Her eyes travelled over the seething mass as she tried to pick out Danny's familiar head of dark hair and she waved one hand as soon as she spotted it.

'Over here, Danny,' she called, wondering if he would hear her above the din.

His deep blue eyes brightened and his mouth stretched in a happy grin and she suddenly noticed that he'd grown up almost overnight. Just a few days ago he was her precious baby preparing for his first day at school and look at him now, so much more self-assured. He even seemed taller in his school uniform.

'Hey, Mum, look at my picture. We did painting today,' said a voice at her elbow as the child she was watching ran right past her without sparing her a glance.

'Hey, Dad, what are you doing here?' he demanded exuberantly. 'Can we go home or have you got to go back to work?'

Sam accepted Danny's offering numbly and wrapped an arm round his shoulders. She gazed blankly at his artistic effort while he explained the significance of the multicoloured swirls and blobs but all she could see was the image of that other face so like her son's.

Jamie, he was called. She'd heard that much as Daniel had greeted him with a matching grin and led him away towards his car, so concentrated on his son's conversation that he hadn't noticed her standing just feet away.

They could almost be twins, Jamie and her son, except Danny was possibly a few months younger.

Her thoughts were turbulent and disjointed as she led the way along the road towards her car.

Most of the other vehicles had gone, now, so there was no one around to notice that she was operating on automatic pilot. Daniel's was nowhere in sight, either—but then, she hadn't known about his son, so she wouldn't have been looking for it in the first place.

The feeling of hurt and disillusionment was overwhelming.

Did that mean it had all been a lie?

All those loving words that she'd believed without question. And all the time that she'd thought they were heading towards a permanent commitment, he'd been seeing someone else, sleeping with someone else, giving someone else his baby.

Sam didn't sleep much that night, and that made her angry.

She was able to keep smiling through the usual morning routine but once she'd dropped Danny off at school it was time for some stern self-appraisal.

She pulled right over to the side of the road and switched off the engine before letting her head drop back against the support. It was only a couple of minutes' drive away from the GP unit but the road skirted the edge of a hill and from her vantage point it seemed almost as if she could see forever.

It had rained several hours ago—she'd been lying awake listening to it—and everywhere had that 'just washed' freshness about it. There was a hawthorn tree growing just inside the stone wall beside her and the tiny white petals were beginning to scatter across the grey stones like miniature confetti.

In the distance there were the scattered white blobs of flocks of sheep busily cropping the new grass on the hills while down in the valley the Eden River meandered its way, glittering as the sun caught it.

She wound down the window and drew in a deep breath. Even the air seemed different around Edenthwaite. Fresh and crisp and full of a myriad unidentified scents and sounds even this early in the year. By the time full summer arrived there would be so many more, all of them familiar from her childhood years and every one of them signifying that elusive mixture that meant she had come home again.

Home again? Just the words were enough to send her thoughts into a spin. Over the years, her relationship with her parents had deteriorated to the point that she'd once thought that she would never be able to come back.

Maturity and motherhood had made her realise that, for all her disapproval of her daughter's conduct, her mother needed her now. She was also convinced that her son would be better off—and safer— growing up here rather than in the centre of a city.

Now that she was here and surrounded by all the things she remembered from her own childhood, she was more convinced than ever that she'd made the right decision…in spite of the fact that she was going to be working with Daniel Hennessy for at least the next six months.

If it all became too much, she could always console herself with the prospect of transferring to another practice in a nearby town at the first available opportunity. It wouldn't be as ideal as Denison

Memorial as far as visiting her mother was concerned, but certainly not as impossible as keeping an eye on her from a hundred or more miles away.

Anyway, more than five years had passed since she and Daniel had last worked together and in spite of her heartbreak she'd managed to get on with her life without him.

What did it matter if she was only now discovering that he'd been two-timing her all those years ago? It was all in the past.

Anyway, rather than harking back it would probably make much more sense if she treated him like a stranger. After all, she really didn't know the man he'd become. He was married now and had a son. It was hardly his fault that she'd started to daydream, wondering if there might be some way for them to recapture what they'd once shared...what she'd *believed* they'd once shared.

It was obvious, now, that he'd been sharing something very similar with at least one other woman and who knew how many more? He'd certainly been good-looking enough to attract plenty of attention, and it was disappointing to find that she'd been taken in so easily. It definitely made the question of telling him about Danny something to think very carefully about. There was no guarantee that Daniel would welcome the news and she wasn't going to set her son up for any more heartache if she could help it.

Still, she had to admit that the roguish dimple was still as potent as ever when attached to a certain smile.

'Enough!' she exclaimed and reached forward to start the engine. It wouldn't do to be late, especially if she was hoping to impress her colleagues enough to make them want to keep her on after Grace was ready to return to work.

'I'm not dead and nor is he,' she declared aloud, the words whipped over her shoulder by the wind rushing in through the open window. 'It's perfectly permissible for me to appreciate a good-looking man. It certainly doesn't mean that I need to do anything about it or there are several actors I could have been stalking for years!'

There was a smile on her face as she drove the last few hundred yards into the car park, put there by the theoretical prospect of having to choose between George Clooney and Pierce Brosnan.

The fact that Pierce Brosnan looked more than a little like a certain local GP had nothing to do with her eventual choice...did it?

CHAPTER FOUR

'NORMAN, is there any chance you could pull a few strings for me?' Sam began as she hurried into the staff room, only to find that Norman wasn't in the room.

Daniel, however, was.

'Norman's had to go and pick Angela up,' he offered, looking up from his perusal of a copy of the local newspaper. 'Her car died on her about a mile out of town and as she's got most of the pictures destined for her next exhibition in the back of it, she didn't dare abandon it to walk to the garage.'

Sam pulled a face. Not at the thought that Norman's wife should have needed him when *she* wanted to talk to him but at the thought that she couldn't get an answer to an urgent problem.

'Does it have to be Norman, or could I help?' Daniel volunteered, much to her surprise. The last week or so she'd seen so little of him that she was convinced he was deliberately avoiding her—not that she'd been wanting to spend time in his company.

'Perhaps you could,' she mused aloud and perched on the arm of the nearest chair. 'Have you come across Philip Morrison?'

'Senior or junior? One's in his teens, keen sportsman and goes to Sedbergh School, and then there's the grandfather he's named after who farms out towards Netherthwaite.'

'You're really getting into this family connections

57

thing, aren't you?' she quipped with a grin. 'It's Philip junior I was talking about. I've just had the results of some x-rays and I need to send him for an emergency referral. I was hoping Norman would know an inside route to getting the fastest possible response.'

'That urgent?' he asked quietly, abandoning the paper completely.

'I'm afraid so, if it's what I think it is.' She gestured with the large envelope in her hand. 'Can I show you?'

'Come through to my room and we'll put it up on the light box,' he suggested, making his way swiftly towards her. 'What were his presenting symptoms?'

'Pain and swelling in his shin, initially. He went to see his doctor at school and was prescribed an anti-inflammatory analgesic. He ran out of tablets while he was home on holiday at Easter so his mother brought him here for a repeat prescription. When I spoke to him, he admitted that the tablets didn't seem to be doing anything. In fact, the pain was steadily growing worse.'

She slid the shadowy film up under the clips and flicked the switch. Instantly the shadows separated themselves into the outline of the young man's lower leg and her eyes were inevitably drawn to the ominous mass a few inches below the knee joint centred in the tibia.

'That looks like a Ewing's sarcoma to me,' she continued grimly as she pointed at the misshapen bone. 'And by my calculations it's been there for at least six months, getting steadily worse.'

'Six months too long for something like this,' Daniel growled as he leant forward for a closer inspection of his own. 'He hardly needs to wait for a CT or MRI scan and a biopsy will only confirm what is blindingly obvious.'

He straightened up and made his way to his desk. 'I'll make a phone call straight away and see what luck I have,' he muttered, his mind already on the task.

Sam perched on the edge of one of the chairs on the opposite side of the desk and waited for the call to go through. She almost smiled when she saw the way he was doodling on his blotter. He'd never been very good at waiting for anything without keeping his hands busy and it was good to see that he hadn't changed…in that, at least.

One half of the blotter was heavily decorated by the time he finished with the last of a long series of calls but he sank back with a satisfied sigh.

'As you've probably gathered, he's going to have to travel to Keighley, but they've got a bed for him tomorrow afternoon and they'll start work on him the following morning.'

'That's brilliant!' she exclaimed, dragging herself out of her prolonged scrutiny. It had been fascinating to watch him and her appreciation of the man he was now had grown with each passing minute. Not that her personal approval made any difference to the situation. 'It only goes to prove that all too often it's not *what* you know but *who* you know that gets things done.'

'Unfortunately, you're right,' he conceded, apparently oblivious to the fact that she'd been watching him avidly for the last quarter of an hour. 'But at least this time knowing someone in that field meant

I could ask all the right questions to get the answer I wanted.'

'Now all we've got to do is break the news to Philip and his family,' Sam pointed out, forcing herself to concentrate. 'That's one part of our job that I really hate, and in this case there isn't really time to bring Philip in for an appointment at the practice.'

'And it's hardly the sort of thing you can break over the phone even if he is surrounded by family. Do you want me to do it?' he offered. 'The Morrisons are almost our nearest neighbours and it would only take me a couple of minutes to make the detour.'

He stood up and began rolling his sleeves down before sliding his arms into his suit jacket.

It felt strangely intimate to watch the man dressing, almost as if she'd strayed into his bedroom, and Sam hastily averted her gaze towards the x-ray view box.

'He's my patient, now that Grace is on maternity leave, so I should be the one to explain what we've found and give him an idea of what's going to happen to him,' she said firmly as she slid the plate into its protective envelope. 'I also need to write a covering note for him to take to Keighley with him tomorrow.'

'How long will that take you?' He shot up his sleeve to look at his watch. 'I've got to collect my son from school in about half an hour. If you want to ride along with me we could both go to the Morrisons to break the news. They're bound to have questions. Then you could join us for supper, if you like.'

Sam was quite taken aback by the invitation. Perhaps he hadn't been deliberately avoiding her all week, otherwise why was he proposing spending more time together unnecessarily?

'Shouldn't you make a phone call to find out if it's convenient to bring a guest at such short notice?' she suggested.

'Mother won't mind,' he said with a dismissive gesture. 'As far as she's concerned, the more the merrier.'

'Your mother? But I thought…' It took that long for her brain to catch up with her mouth but from the knowing expression on his face she could see that it was already too late. He knew what she'd been going to say. Why hadn't she realised at the time that the Mrs Hennessy who had phoned him at the GP unit could equally well be his mother as his wife?

'Unlike you, I've never married,' he said gruffly, the words sounding so strangely bleak that they made her heart ache. 'There's no wife to object if I bring extra mouths to feed at short notice. How about you? Will your husband worry if you're late home?'

Sam's brain was still trying to unscramble the co-nundrum of a man with a son who had never had a wife. The expression in his eyes was enough to tell her that there was a sad story attached to the situation but it was also telling her that he didn't choose to tell her any more than he had.

'I'm divorced,' she said bluntly, not seeing any point in covering the fact up. Her mother had been trying to persuade her to skirt round the issue so her parents' friends didn't find out the shameful fact of their daughter's failure. Sam was determined not to live with any more lies if she could help it. It had been bad enough struggling through the marriage itself knowing that she'd made a mistake, without compounding the situation by pretending she was happy.

If she had to pretend, she'd far rather her mother pretended that the marriage had never taken place, but that would brand her only grandchild a bastard, which was even worse.

Daniel didn't comment but he hadn't been able to control the eyebrows that shot up in reaction to her statement.

'So, does that mean you're free to join us?' he asked mildly.

Part of her would still like nothing better than to spend time in the man's company, especially now she knew that he wasn't married. At least the fact that he was willing to bring up his son was further proof that he wasn't the type of man to deliberately abandon her five years ago.

Unfortunately, if she were to go with him, she would have to reveal the existence of her son…*their* son…and until she'd had time to think this new situation through she was going to keep the two of them well apart.

'I'm sorry, but I can't. As it is I'll be pushed to get back in time for a prior engagement this evening.'

It wasn't just an excuse she'd conjured out of thin air. She'd actually promised Danny that she would take him for a quick visit to his grandmother after he'd had his tea and she was determined not to break her word.

With the rift that her pregnancy and divorce had caused, he'd had little time to get to know the older woman and she was keen to start to remedy the situation. It would probably be a war of attrition and could take as long as drips of water wearing away a stone, but it would never happen if the first drop didn't fall.

As time went on, Sam had grown more and more aware that their family consisted of just the three of them and she'd become almost superstitious about the need to let Danny get to know his grandmother before she went for her hip-replacement surgery. Not that Sam was expecting anything to go wrong, but still…

'Perhaps another time, then,' he said with a distinct chill in his voice. 'Would you rather I didn't go to the Morrisons with you, either?'

Sam did some swift calculations. She would need to make a phone call to find out if it was possible, but if she picked Danny up as usual, she could drop him off with one of the other mothers until she returned from her visit to the farm. Life would be so much easier if she was in the same position as Daniel, with his mother available for the majority of school runs.

The logistics of the situation today would probably be less fraught if she went alone but, since he'd offered, the last thing she wanted was to blight the first tender shoots of a friendly relationship between the two of them by refusing his company.

'If I meet you there it means I'll have my own car to get back home,' she pointed out, then gave a silent sigh of relief when he nodded his agreement.

'Shall we say half-past four at the gate to the farm? I take it you know the way?'

Sam slowed down slightly as she passed Daniel's house. Not enough that someone inside the house would notice, but just enough to have a good look at it.

It looked as if it had once been a little row of farm labourers' cottages that had been converted into a single property and extended. It certainly wasn't big or impressive but gave the impression that inside would be comfortable and cosy whatever the weather threw at it.

'A shame they didn't use the same architect when they modernised *my* cottage,' she grumbled, remembering the ugly lean-to extension at the back that housed the kitchen and a very cramped bathroom up above. The fact that Danny had to wander through her bedroom every time he wanted to use the bathroom had turned into an excuse for bouncing on her bed. The room just wasn't big enough for that, to say nothing of the wear and tear on the springs. It also meant she could never be guaranteed any privacy, and this alone would be the main reason why she would look for alternative accommodation as soon as she knew whether she would be staying on in six months' time.

As she pulled through the farm gate she found Daniel waiting for her and they continued up the drive in convoy.

'They're expecting us,' he said quietly as she climbed out of her car to join him. 'I timed my call for milking time and left a brief message on their answering machine.'

If she'd thought about it, she could have done the same, but it was going to take more than a few days to get back into country ways again. Once upon a time she'd have known such things as the time a local farmer did his milking.

'Two doctors!' exclaimed a voice and they turned to see the elder Philip Morrison walking towards them, his tall spare figure typical of local stock. 'Good job us don't have to pay by the visit these days or us'd have to sell the farm to pay the bill.'

He shook Daniel's hand then turned to fix Sam with eyes the same clear pale grey of a moorland mist.

'I know you, lass,' he said with a broad welcoming grin. 'You're Doc Denison's daughter, aren't you? Good to see you've come home to Edenthwaite at last.'

For a moment Sam was startled that she'd been recognised. She'd been half-afraid that locals would have treated her a little more warily in view of the fact that she'd been away so long. But then all she was conscious of was a deep warm glow at his ready acceptance.

'Thank you, Mr Morrison,' she said as she shook the gnarled hand. 'It's great to be back. I hadn't realised how much I'd missed it.'

'It's the air, lass,' he confided. 'Around here it's as addictive as good wine. People born to it don't fare nearly so well anywhere else.'

'Philip? Was that the doctor?' called a voice from somewhere just inside the farmhouse and they all turned to watch the arrival of a woman just as lean but only half the height of her husband.

'You're not keeping him out here gossiping while I've got a pot of tea ready for pouring!' she exclaimed then did a double take. 'Sam Denison, is that you, lass? Well, bless my old boots!'

She bustled forward to fling her arms round Sam

in a brief heartfelt hug, her smile even wider than her husband's if that was possible.

'Why didn't that grandson of mine tell me that you were the doctor he'd been seeing? The last time you were around here was when you were bridesmaid at our niece Sarah's wedding and I'm sure I'd have remembered if young Philip had said that there was another Denison come to work at the surgery.'

'I've only been back for a couple of days and he probably didn't mention it because I'm not called Denison any more. I'm Dr Taylor now,' she explained, suddenly feeling guilty that she hadn't kept in better contact with all the old friends of her childhood. This whole family had once treated her as if she was almost a direct blood relative. It wouldn't have cost her much in time or effort to have made a call or written a letter at least once in a while.

'Nay, lass. You were born a Denison and you'll stay a Denison. You mark my words. Local folk know their own. Now come along inside and let me get you a cup of tea.'

She bustled back into the farmhouse and they all meekly trooped in after her.

'I asked if you knew the way here,' Daniel muttered in her ear as he brought up the rear. 'Why didn't you tell me that you're practically a family member?'

'Because I'm not,' she hissed back keeping one eye on where she was going while she tried to throw him an indignant look and all the while trying to ignore the sudden shiver of awareness raising the hairs on the back of her neck. 'I haven't seen any of them since I left home to go to medical school.'

There was no time for any further conversation as

they were welcomed by the gathered throng congregated in the cosy farmhouse kitchen.

In no time at all they were seated at the enormous wooden table with steaming mugs of tea in front of them and had been regaled with a potted history of the family's doings ever since Sam last visited.

There was a sudden pause in the noise and laughter and Sam barely had time for a single breath before Philip Morrison cleared his throat.

'Now, then. I've never believed in dancing around when something needed saying,' he began, and everyone grew still. 'You might call it taking the bull by the horns, but much as we love you, lass, we know this wasn't just a social visit.'

Sam dragged her gaze away from the pale grey eyes set in that kindly face and threw an uncertain look in Daniel's direction.

''Tis probably not the way it's done in hospitals and such,' he continued firmly, 'but in this family we believe in facing things together. So, what's the verdict on young Philip? Is it cancer in his leg? Will he have to have it cut off?'

Sam didn't know whether to laugh or cry. Knowing the family so well, she should have realised that this would happen.

She turned to face young Philip and realised that at some time in the last half an hour his parents had manoeuvred themselves until they were sitting on either side of him.

She saw his mother slide a supporting arm around him and it didn't look out of place for all that the seventeen-year-old was now nearly twice her size. Philip, himself, was meeting her gaze full on, for all that there was fear in his eyes.

'The x-rays show that there *is* something going on in the bone,' she confirmed honestly, knowing that it was the only way to deal with this family. 'We need to take a sample of the bone to find out exactly what it is, but we're already pretty certain that it's what's called a Ewing's sarcoma.'

'How bad is it, lass?' Philip senior prompted in a voice husky with concern.

'It's most common in young men between the ages of ten and twenty, and the new treatments developed over the last few years mean that more than sixty per cent of them are cured.'

Silently, she added that his odds would have been even better if he'd been referred six months ago when the pain first started, but she couldn't burden them with that. They were going to have to deal with the situation in front of them without thinking of 'what if'.

'Cured by cutting the leg off?' Philip junior prompted, taking the initiative from the family for the first time.

'Very rarely,' she admitted bluntly, 'and then only if the first line of attack fails. The first stage will be to get an accurate diagnosis from a biopsy—tests done on a small sample taken out of the tumour. There'll be scans done to establish exactly how much of the bone is involved and then the form of treatment will be decided.'

'Depending on the severity,' Daniel cut in, giving her the chance to get her voice under control again. She hoped he was the only one who had noticed how her emotions had started to take over. It was so hard when she could remember teasing Philip about how sweet he looked in his pageboy outfit. 'You'll probably have a combination of radiation therapy and chemotherapy but, even if surgery *is* necessary, it's unlikely that you'll lose your leg. In fact you could end up with a leg worth almost as much as the whole farm, because they can now do replacements of whole sections of bone with titanium.'

'Metal? You mean like the hollow tin legs they used to give the airmen after the war?'

'Nothing like that, thank goodness,' said Daniel with a chuckle. 'Titanium is a very lightweight but super-strong metal. It's inert, so it can't play host to infection but, more than that, it's very special because it can actually fuse with human bone. Once it's fitted into the space left by cutting out a tumour, it will actually become part of the remaining bone and will allow muscle and skin to grow over it. They've even been able to use it to reconstruct people's faces after horrendous accidents.'

'Anyway, we don't know yet whether you'll need that,' Sam continued, her emotions and her voice under control again now that she was concentrating on the specifics. 'If you're lucky, the chemo and radiotherapy will do the job.'

'But at least I know that they're not the end of the road,' young Philip said and straightened his shoulders. 'Anyway, I have no intention of letting this thing beat me. I'm a good cricketer and I have every intention of going after a place on a team at national level, even if I don't make it to Internationals. I might not be fit enough to make it *this* year, but I'll be there next year, for certain.'

Sam was fighting tears by the time he finished and she was surprised but not a little grateful to feel

Daniel's hand squeeze hers under cover of the table.

'In which case, there's obviously not a minute to lose,' Daniel said, the fact that his voice was noticeably rougher than usual was the only way that Sam could tell he was similarly affected. 'It's a good job we managed to get you an appointment for tomorrow.'

They were there for another half an hour going over the specifics and making their farewells and Sam was completely exhausted by the time she climbed back into her car.

A tap on the window beside her head nearly made her jump out of her skin.

'Sorry about that,' Daniel said when she wound the window down. Are you sure you haven't got time to stop off for a cup of coffee?'

For a moment the caring expression in his eyes almost made her change her mind, but then she remembered who would be waiting to meet her when she got there.

'I'm sure,' she said, the pain of his deceit washing over her again and adding an edge to her voice. 'I need to get back. Thank you for asking.'

She put the car into gear and pulled away muttering to herself. 'Thank you for asking! Wouldn't Mother be pleased to hear the party manners?'

Still, she could hardly have said that she didn't want to have her nose rubbed in the fact that he'd been two-timing her five years ago while she'd been falling in love with him. It was hard enough seeing those familiar deep blue eyes and dark hair every time she looked at Danny without having to face his double.

*   *   *

'I'm big enough to do it myself,' Danny declared and Sam barely suppressed a groan.

That was fast becoming his favourite phrase, since he'd started school, although why it hadn't happened sooner, while he was attending playgroup, she had no idea.

It was becoming something of a minefield sorting out which battles to fight and which to concede. This looked as if it was one of the latter.

'You remember that you need to test the temperature of the water before you climb in?' she asked, hoping she sounded totally unworried by the prospect of letting a five-year-old loose in a bathroom to draw his own bath.

'Of course,' he said dismissively, already making for the stairs as he sensed her capitulation. 'I'm not a baby any more. And anyway, I'm a boy. We have sep'rate bathrooms for boys and girls at school and the girls aren't allowed in.'

Sam suppressed a pang at this further evidence that her baby was growing up fast and hovered at the foot of the stairs for a moment. From there she could follow his progress into her bedroom and through to the bathroom.

There was silence for a moment and then the familiar sound of water gushing into the bath.

Knowing that she would be better able to judge what was happening from directly underneath, she hurried through to the kitchen and switched off the radio she'd left playing.

Every minute passed interminably until the sound of running water ceased, to be replaced by the familiar splashing sounds of a child playing his usual games with the flotilla of boats and menagerie of water monsters.

Happy that one danger point had passed, she opened the oven door to check on the chicken casserole reheating inside. Not long, now, before it was ready. All she had to do was mash the potatoes and drain the carrots.

With a hot meal provided at school, Danny didn't really need a large meal at this time of day, but she needed to cook for herself and actually enjoyed the time they spent at the table together. She got to hear all the specifics of his eventful days and made sure that he wasn't allowing any minor problems to grow out of proportion.

'Danny! Supper will be ready in five minutes!' she called from the foot of the stairs. 'Do you want me to check that you've washed behind your ears before you let the water out?'

There was a beat of silence before he replied followed by the sound of frantic splashing and she grinned. She could easily imagine that he had been hastily hunting for the flannel for a rapid application over the relevant portions of his anatomy.

'I've done it myself,' he called back. 'And I washed my face.'

Sam sighed, wondering how thorough the job had been. This would have been one of the times when it would have been handy to have a man about the place...

The familiar thought brought her up short when she realised that the man she had imagined in the role was Daniel.

For so many years, now, it had been a hopeless fantasy, believing that he had died. Now it was more a case of what *might* have been, and what probably *was* happening in that cosy-looking home she'd passed this evening.

Was he, even now, helping his other son to don his pyjamas, relishing the time they spent together at the end of a busy day? She was sure there must be many things that father and son would share that wouldn't be revealed to female members of the family. Secret discussions about what terrible creatures *girls* were and what a trial it was for boys to have to put up with them. Tips and hints about the best way to kick a ball and…

'I'm ready!' Danny announced as he bounded down the stairs towards her, his pyjama jacket buttoned askew and his damp hair sticking up like a demented hedgehog. 'What are we having to eat? Is it that chicken stew thing? We had chicken legs at school today and I picked mine up and chewed at it like a dog. The teacher said it was all right to pick it up because chickens can fly. She said we mustn't pick up bones of other meat because cows can't fly. They would need very big wings, wouldn't they, Mum? When I finished eating there was only the bone left.'

'Well, I'm glad you didn't eat the bone or you wouldn't have room for your food now,' she said with a smile. She would have loved to wrap this bright, cheerful, amazing child of hers tightly in her arms but confined herself to smoothing her hand over the spiky hair.

'Oh, Daniel James! Your hair's still full of shampoo!' she exclaimed.

'It doesn't matter, does it? It's clean.' He turned

those big blue eyes up to her with a pleading expression. 'And I'm starving.'

'If you don't rinse the shampoo out it will make your hair all sticky and it could make the skin on your head sore.' The expression on his face told her that he wasn't willing to concede, so she brought out the big guns.

'It could even make your hair fall out in chunks,' she warned, putting a hand on his shoulder to guide him back upstairs again.

'But I've already let the water out,' he whined in a typical five-year-old way.

'It won't take long if I use the hand shower thing over the edge of the bath. You could just take your pyjama top off so it didn't get wet. Then you could set the table for me while I serve everything out.'

'OK,' he surrendered and picked up his pace, still young enough to relish the responsibility of being given a job to do without seeing it as a chore. 'Will we need spoons as well or is it just knives and forks?'

By the time she followed him into the kitchen a few minutes later they had negotiated a compromise over the night-time bathing ritual. He would be responsible for drawing his own water while she would be responsible for checking that he'd rinsed all the soap off.

She settled down to her meal wondering if this was the start of a trend, now that he was beginning to grow up. Were all little boys like this? Did they all want to take control over their lives, whether they were old enough or not?

It was one thing to have all the book knowledge attendant on her GP qualification, but she was learning that it was another matter entirely to be dealing with motherhood on a daily basis.

So far she'd had an easy ride because he was such an amenable child, but there was no guarantee that couldn't change—not that it would change her love for him if it did, she thought as she listened to him telling one of his action figures about his day.

That was what it was all about, when she came down to the bottom line, Sam thought when she finally collapsed into bed. Whatever she did, her life was going to be full of ups and downs.

She'd fallen in love with Daniel only to lose him, and now that she'd found him again, she'd discovered that he hadn't even been hers in the first place. But out of their relationship she'd acquired Danny, the precious son who was now the centre of her little universe.

Yes, she'd had her share of heartbreak and disappointment over the last five years, but it was all worth it when she considered what she'd been given in exchange.

CHAPTER FIVE

'PHONE call for you, Sam,' said the voice in her ear. 'I know you were hoping to get away on time but… It seems like a real cry for help. She's almost too upset to be coherent except for demanding to speak to you.'

'Put her through.' What else could she say? It was almost the first time in a week that her list hadn't run over and she'd been intending taking Danny to the swimming pool when she collected him from school.

Still, this was definitely part of the job and there was no point in wasting time trying to second-guess the situation when she had no information to work on.

There was a click as the line was opened followed by the sound of muffled sobbing.

'Hello? This is Dr Taylor here. Can I help?'

It took several seconds for the person on the other end to respond, and from her voice it was evident that she was fighting panic. 'Oh, Doctor, he tried to do it,' the voice quavered in the end. 'I was so afraid he was going to, and he did.'

'I'm sorry.' Sam was completely at a loss. 'Who am I speaking to? The receptionist didn't tell me your name.'

'Ashland,' the voice said with a gulp, obviously fighting for control. 'It's Mrs Ashland. Do you remember me?'

Instantly Sam had a mental image of the heavily pregnant woman, one of her very first patients when she joined the practice. She'd offered a listening ear to the poor woman's troubled husband, but since then she'd only heard at second hand how her pregnancy was progressing.

Obviously the situation had reached crisis point.

'Do you mean your husband has hurt himself?' she asked, trying to keep her voice gentle in spite of the urgency. 'Do you want me to call an ambulance?'

'No! Don't call an ambulance. He's all right… Well, no, he's not all right. Oh, Doctor, I don't know what to do. I'm at my wits' end. I went out to the barn to call him in for a phone call and I found him…' The words halted and Sam heard the sound of a painful swallow. 'He was tying a rope over one of the beams in the barn. Well, he was trying to, but with only one hand…'

She gave a broken laugh that verged on hysteria. 'Stupid, isn't it? He's lost his hand so he wants to kill himself but he couldn't do it because he's lost his hand.'

'Shh! Shh!' Sam soothed. 'Think of the baby, Mrs Ashland. It won't do him any good if you let yourself get in such a state.'

Mention of her unborn child seemed to have the desired effect as Janet's frenzied laughter died away into a subdued sob.

'Now, you said he didn't manage to tie the rope. Does this mean that you've brought him into the house with you? Is he somewhere safe?' Nightmare visions of the poor man finally succeeding at his grim endeavour while his wife spoke to the doctor filled her head.

'He's sitting in the kitchen with a cup of tea. I've given him some of his pain tablets but he says they don't do any good. *Nothing* does any good. Please, Dr Taylor. *Please* can you come and talk to him? There must be something you can do to stop him killing himself.'

A few minutes later Sam came off the phone with her head whirling.

The only way she'd managed to calm her pregnant patient down was to promise to come out to the farm. Now, all she had to do was arrange for someone to collect her son from school and look after him until she returned from her visit.

'Mara, I've got a problem,' she announced as she deposited a pile of patient files on the receptionists' desk. She grimaced when she caught sight of the time. She'd promised to get out to the Ashlands' farm as soon as possible but time was marching on.

'That phone call?' Mara Frost threw her a worried look. 'Do you want me to see if one of the other doctors is free? Do you need to confer?'

'No. It's not that sort of problem. I need to go out on an urgent home visit, but I've left it too late to get hold of any of the other mothers to ask if they'll pick up my son from school.'

The sound behind her wasn't very loud but it was enough to tell her that there was someone standing behind her. She glanced over her shoulder and found herself looking straight into Daniel's eyes.

'Your son?' he echoed, sounding quite shocked. 'I didn't know you had any children.'

'Just the one,' she confirmed, frustrated that this had happened now. She hadn't realised that Daniel hadn't heard about her son but did he have to learn about him at this precise moment? She didn't have time for this conversation, not while she had a frantic patient waiting for her to arrive.

There was a strange uncomfortable silence, almost as if each of them was waiting for the other to speak, then Mara broke in.

'You're just off to get Jamie, aren't you, Daniel?' she said brightly and Sam could have groaned. She could see exactly what was coming with the inevitability of a runaway train. 'Would you be able to pick Sam's son up at the same time? Your mother wouldn't mind an extra body, would she? Then Sam could collect him from you when she finishes.'

It was an obvious solution but Sam wished there was almost any other alternative.

Over the short space of time since she'd come home she'd been unable to avoid learning more about the man Daniel had become over the last five years.

At first she'd been reluctant to admit that both he and his son were entitled to know of each other's existence, but deep down she knew it was right. Never in her wildest dreams had she imagined that it would happen in this way.

'What do you say?' he threw the words at her almost as a challenge. 'Will you trust me with your son?'

She almost laughed at the irony of the question.

'Of course,' she said flatly, knowing she had no option and wishing she could be in two places at once.

Her mother's instincts were screaming at her. Like most five-year-olds Danny would probably be completely oblivious to anything but the excitement of spending time with his friend. But what effect would it have on Danny if he were to suddenly realise that this man was his real father? Would he understand that Jamie was his half-brother? She should be there with him for such a potentially traumatic event; to be on hand to give him some sort of explanation that his five-year-old mind could grasp.

But there wasn't time for that, not if she was to get to Mrs Ashland within the time she'd promised.

'I need to phone the school to let them know it's all right to release him to your care,' she said shakily, reaching for the instrument on the desk. All she could do was hope that the staff wouldn't make some comment in front of the two children. Their likeness to each other and to the man in front of her was so strong that seeing all three of them together might make the connection that had been missing until now.

'I'll be back as soon as I can,' she promised as they parted company outside the door to walk to their respective cars.

'No hurry,' he said with a dismissive wave, apparently recovered from his shock at her unknown motherhood. 'My mother will be in her element. She gets on very well with little boys. Says she had more than enough practice when I was small.'

That was before she realised that she had another grandson, Sam thought as she deposited her bag on the seat beside her and pulled the door shut. I hope she's got a strong heart because there's a shock coming her way.

All thoughts of the meeting taking place at the school had to be firmly pushed to the back of her mind when she drew up outside the Ashlands' farmhouse.

'Oh, Dr Taylor, I'm so glad you're here!' Janet's body was far too ungainly for hurrying and her face was still blotchy with the evidence of her recent tears but she came out to meet Sam in the yard. 'Please, come into the house.'

'Does your husband know you phoned me?' Sam was just a little uncomfortable making this visit. Mark Ashland wasn't officially her patient, but since his wife's first visit to the surgery she'd been hoping that he would contact her.

She'd actually done some research into the different drug options that could be used to try to minimise the pain experienced with the phenomenon of phantom limbs and had even caught the tail end of a television programme that had mentioned the problem.

None of that would be of any use if the man refused to speak to her.

'I told him,' Janet Ashland said with more than a hint of pure North Country stubbornness as she led the way into the old-fashioned farmhouse kitchen. 'Ever since he came out of hospital he's been trying to cope by himself. Wouldn't let either side of the family help, even though we've both got brothers and, once I got so big, I couldn't help much any more, either. And this is the easiest time at the moment. What about lambing next spring? Well, enough's enough. I told him he had two choices. Either he would see you willingly, or he'd see you unwillingly. One or t'other.'

She was clearly caught between anger and tears as she reached for a mug with a large cheerful sunflower painted on the outside. 'Can I pour you some tea?'

Sam nodded distractedly, her gaze already fixed on the desperate-looking man hunched at one end of the table.

With a smile on his face she could imagine that he would have been very good-looking. He certainly had the tall, broad-shouldered physique to turn heads. Somehow, that made his present state of collapse all the more poignant.

'I'd love a cup of tea but, as for anything else, that's up to your husband,' she said quietly. 'He's an adult and is therefore responsible for making his own decisions and I can't force him to talk to me.'

'But…'

Sam held up her hand to silence the interruption and directed her words to the silent man.

'Well, Mr Ashland,' she challenged softly. 'Are you willing to talk?'

She had to hold her breath for a long time while she waited for his reply.

'For all the bloody good it'll do,' he growled as he met her eyes for the first time. For a second she had a flashback of an incident in her childhood when she'd come across some children throwing stones at a cornered dog. There had been the same mute overwhelming misery in the old animal's eyes, too.

Suddenly Mark shot up out of his seat, sending the chair toppling over with a loud clatter onto the flagstoned floor.

'It's a waste of time! All the talking in the world isn't going to help take the pain away, and I just can't live with it any more!' he exclaimed roughly. 'If it was cancer you could cut it out, but how can you cut off a hand that isn't there any more?'

Sam stayed silent when his outburst ended and the

three of them were frozen into a strange sort of tab-leau.

She had both hands clasped tightly round the han-dle of her bag, the weight braced against the front of her thighs. Janet was over by the solid-fuel range, her eyes wide and fearful and one trembling hand pressed over her mouth as she watched her husband.

Mark was standing like a young Colossus with his legs braced in a fighting stance with one hand clenched into a fist.

Slowly Sam drew in a breath, silently praying that she would find the right words at the right time. This situation was a disaster just waiting to happen—a powder keg primed to explode and destroy at least two lives.

'Does talking make it worse?' she asked quietly and sighed in relief when she saw his shoulders drop.

'To be honest, Doctor, I don't know what makes it worse and what makes it better,' he admitted wea-rily. 'If I did, I might be able to cope with it better. I just feel so helpless.'

'And a man your size isn't used to feeling help-less,' she guessed. 'I'm betting that all your life you've been healthy and hearty and usually bigger and brawnier than anyone else around. *And* accus-tomed to working the rest of them into the ground.'

'You're not wrong,' his wife exclaimed proudly. 'He's always been a hard worker. Does the work of two most days.'

'Not any more,' he said dully, reaching for the chair and setting it upright again. 'I just can't do it any more without my hand, and with the little one due any day...' He let the sentence hang in the air with a shake of his head.

'So, just for the sake of argument, are you willing to sit down and drink a cup of tea with me while we talk things through?' Sam suggested. 'I'm not saying I can make any difference, but we'll never know if I don't try.'

He paused for a moment before nodding towards the chair nearest to her. It was grudging, but it was a capitulation of sorts.

To take the edge off the atmosphere she started a conversation about the soon-to-be-born baby and was treated to a special view of the new cot.

It was a work of art obviously destined to become a family heirloom, the wood shaped and polished to perfection. Even the rockers were decorated, and so well designed that the whole thing moved perfectly quietly and smoothly.

The bedding, too, was hand-made, this time by the mother-to-be. There was old-fashioned tatted lace around the edges of the sheets and delicate embroidery in each corner, all done under the instruction of Janet's grandmother who had insisted on passing on her own skills down the family.

In spite of the fact that making such a cot would probably be beyond Mark in his present condition, all three of them carefully avoided referring to it.

It was nearly half an hour later that Sam judged it was time to call a halt to their temporary truce.

'So, Mark Ashland, are you going to let me examine your stump?' she asked bluntly.

He blinked. 'Why would you want to do that? When the pain started I was convinced that something had been left inside during the operation. But the surgeon took x-ray pictures of it to check. He says it's all healed now, and there's nothing wrong with it.'

'I just want to check something out. It will only take a minute or two,' she added persuasively.

Reluctantly, he began to unbutton his shirt. When Janet would have got up to help him, Sam waved her away.

'To quote my five-year-old son, he's a big boy, Janet. He can manage his buttons himself, especially when it's just undoing them. I bet he never had any trouble getting you out of your clothes with either hand.'

She'd startled a chuckle out of both of them and was touched to see that they both blushed, too.

'It's a bit like a child learning to do things for the first time,' she pointed out. 'It's slow and they get very frustrated but, if you keep leaping in to do it for them, your child will be the only adult in Edenthwaite who has to have his mummy do his shoes up for him.'

'But…' She clearly wasn't convinced.

'It's exactly the same thing, I promise you,' she said gently. 'We learn things by doing them over and over again until we can do them automatically without thinking about every stage. A bit like learning to change gear when you're learning to drive a car. At first you can't get the sequence of hand and foot movements in the right order and you nearly crash, taking your eyes off the road to see what you're doing. But by the time you take your test your brain has stored the information so that it can do it without you having to think about it.'

'That makes sense,' Mark said grudgingly, distracted from what she was doing by the conversation.

'It's taken ages for me to be able to brush my teeth without getting the toothpaste up my nose and all down my chin, but I don't make any mess, now.'

'That means that, gradually, you're teaching your brain new skills and, over time, your control will get better and better.' This was always an important point to stress, especially to someone who had been such an expert craftsman. He might never achieve one hundred per cent of his former skill with his right hand, as that had been controlled by the dominant side of his brain. But he certainly wouldn't be what the locals called 'cack-handed' forever.

'That's all well and good, but what can I do about the pain?' he demanded, bringing the conversation back to his original problem. 'How is it that a hand that isn't there any more can cause me so much pain?'

'If you'll let me, I'll try to demonstrate,' Sam suggested. 'Can you feel me touching the skin on the end of your stump?' She stroked over the neat skin flap that had been fashioned to cover the wound.

'Yes, I can,' he reported.

'How about here?' She touched closer to one of the main scars.

'Yes…but it's different. It feels almost as if you're touching one of my missing fingers. My thumb, in fact.' He stared at her in amazement. 'How did you do that?'

'*I* didn't do it. Your brain did.' Sam reached for her bag and took out a pad of paper to draw a rough representation of a human brain with 'wiring' leading out to various parts of the body. 'Your hand used to send messages to a particular set of places in your brain and it used to receive instructions in return.'

'You mean like, that's hot, take your hand away from it?' Janet suggested.

'Exactly like that,' Sam agreed. 'But when a limb isn't there any more, scientists have found that it doesn't mean that part of the brain shuts down. Quite often it means that other neighbouring areas start "squatting" in the area that isn't being used any more. Unfortunately, that can mean that your brain gets some of its signals crossed and thinks the messages are coming from a hand that isn't there any more.'

'So how do I stop it?' he demanded. 'Do I have to have part of my brain cut out?'

'Because there's no such thing as a wiring diagram of a brain, that would be very difficult to do without risking damaging other important areas. It's especially difficult as no two people are exactly the same.'

'So does that mean I'm stuck with this forever?' he challenged. 'Because I'm telling you, I don't think I can stand it. Can you imagine what it would be like to have your hand clenched into a tight fist twenty-four hours a day? It's been like it for weeks and months and the pain just never lets up.'

Sam had to fight to stop the smile that wanted to lift the corners of her mouth. Until now, Mark hadn't said exactly what form his torment took and she'd been almost dreading asking him. The phenomenon he had just described was so similar to the one she'd seen on the television that she was amazed.

'Mark, are you game to try a little experiment?' she prompted. 'It's something that might seem very silly, and there's no guarantee that it will work, but...'

'Why not? What have I got to lose?' he demanded, but she noticed that the expression in his eyes had slowly been changing. There was far more of a spark in them now than the defeated man he'd been less than an hour ago. It might be a temporary situation, but she was going to do her best to find some way to help.

'Janet, have you got a cardboard box I can use...one that you don't mind me cutting up?'

'What size? A cereal box, or an apple box like we carry the groceries home in?'

'The apple box will be perfect. And a bread knife, too, for cutting some holes.' She unlatched her bag and drew out the large, square mirror she'd been carrying round for nearly ten days. In a few minutes she was going to find out if it had been worth the extra weight.

It didn't take long to saw two holes into the front of the box, each just big enough to fit halfway up Mark's forearms. The right side of the top was left with its flaps intact, but the left side had them cut away so that Mark could look down onto his left hand while his right stump was hidden away.

The mirror was placed on its edge in the middle of the box so that it would reflect his good left hand while completely hiding his missing right one.

'Right, Mark,' she began when all the preparations were finished, carefully choosing her words to start building up the illusion inside his mind that he still had two healthy hands. 'Without looking at them, I want you to put your *two* hands inside the box, one through each hole. Then I want you to clench them both tightly into fists then open your eyes and look into the box.'

She didn't know about the other couple but she was holding her breath as he followed her instructions.

With his eyes tightly closed he slid both arms into the holes, his wife guiding him in the right direction to start.

When his visible hand clenched into a white-knuckled fist he paused, almost as if afraid to take the next step.

'Open your eyes, love,' Janet whispered, excitement mixed with awe in her voice when she caught sight of the illusion. 'Look at your hands!'

Having grown accustomed to looking down at himself and seeing the stump where his hand used to be, it was obviously quite an emotional moment when Mark looked into the box and saw not only his left hand but the reflection of it. With the two hands, real and reflected, side by side, it looked as if his missing hand had miraculously returned.

'Keep both your hands clenched and stay very still for a moment,' Sam said, careful that her words didn't break the illusion. She was finding it very difficult to keep her voice under control, she wanted so much for this to work. 'Let your brain take in what it's seeing, because we're treating it to some of its own medicine. It's been playing a rotten trick on you, so now we're returning the favour.'

She threw a quick glance in Janet's direction and found her face wet with tears.

'You can feel all your muscles and tendons keeping both your hands tightly clenched. Now, slowly uncurl the fingers of ''both'' hands at once and give them a good stretch.'

All three of them were riveted to the sight of two

hands uncurling at the exact same moment side by side.

'Bloody hell!' Mark swore, his face a picture of incredulity. 'Bloody hell, it's a miracle. It's working.'

As they watched, he slowly stretched his fingers out as far as they would go and turned his hand this way and that.

'My hand's open,' he exclaimed. '*Both* my hands are open. I can see them!'

'What about the pain?' Sam prompted softly as she mopped her own tears before her face grew as wet as Janet's. 'Can you take both hands out of the box, now?'

It was almost a shock to see his right arm ending in a stump after the last few minutes of looking at a pair of healthy hands.

'It's gone!' He gazed up at her in disbelief. 'The pain's gone. How did you do that?'

'I didn't. It was your brain that did it,' she pointed out. 'There was no guarantee that it would work and, because everyone's wiring is different, there's no way of knowing how long the effect will last.'

'But I now know for certain that there's nothing wrong with the arm, and if it gets bad again I can have another go at fooling my brain.'

'Well, my contribution will be the mirror,' Sam announced with a watery smile. 'You can keep it as long as you like, with my compliments.'

'How can we ever thank you?' Janet whispered, still overcome. 'If it hadn't been for you...'

'As far as I'm concerned, the most important thing you two can do is make certain to keep talking to each other,' she advised. 'You're a lovely couple, soon to be a family and this is only one of the problems you're going to face together. Just make certain that you *do* face them together, and there won't be many things that can defeat you.'

She turned to pick up her bag. 'Well, that's the end of the sermon for tonight. It's time I went and collected my son and took him home.'

Just those few words were enough to take the shine off the success of the last half an hour.

She'd actually completely forgotten that while she was here trying to help the Ashlands her son was meeting his father for the first time.

What had Daniel thought when he met Danny face to face? What had he said?

He could hardly miss the fact that she had given her son his father's name, nor that Danny was almost the twin of his other son.

And what about Jamie? Apparently, the fact that the two of them had been attending the same school had only occasioned amusement that he and Danny shared the same first names.

She sat in her car for a moment, very tempted to laugh out loud. Only the thought that the Ashlands might be watching kept the impulse under control.

That didn't stop her voicing her thought out loud.

'There are three of them,' she said with a slightly hysterical giggle. 'Three dark-haired, blue-eyed males all called Daniel James. One is known as Daniel, one as Jamie and the other as Danny.'

She set the car in motion, forcing herself to concentrate on her driving rather than her increasingly anxious thoughts. This would not be a good time to lose control of the car or cause an accident. Her precious son had already spent nearly two hours with his father, grandmother and half-brother.

Now it was time to face up to her own problems, and she already knew that she couldn't solve them by using tricks with mirrors.

CHAPTER SIX

'COME in, my dear. You must be Sam,' said an older woman with the same deep blue eyes and dark hair as her son and grandsons', albeit that hers was liberally streaked with grey. 'Somehow I feel that we should have met a long time ago.'

Sam gave her a sharp glance, expecting to see the same censure in her expression that she'd received from her own parents, but couldn't detect any…just a quiet all-encompassing acceptance that warmed her inside.

In spite of that, she stepped over the threshold reluctantly, every nerve stretched tight as she waited for an angry Daniel to appear.

'Mrs Hennessy…' she began hesitantly, not absolutely certain what she wanted to say. It was so unlike her, these days. After the disastrous choices she'd made over the last five years she'd had to become accustomed to fighting her own corner.

Unfortunately, all her courage seemed to have deserted her, especially when she tried to imagine Daniel's reaction to Danny's existence.

Not that she thought he was small-minded enough to take it out on her son. *He* was the only blameless one in the whole situation. But, having seen the cold quiet anger of which Daniel was capable, she had a feeling that he was going to insist on a confrontation.

Logically, she knew that he probably had a right to be angry. He was going to demand why she hadn't told him about her son as soon as she learned that it was his brother who had died.

At the moment, her own anger was directed mainly at herself because all she really wanted to do was grab Danny and disappear.

That was the coward's way out and, with Joyce Hennessy being so unexpectedly welcoming, it obviously wasn't an option.

Daniel's mother took pity on her.

'The boys are in the living room.' She gestured towards the back of the house. 'They've been fed and watered and are now watching something brightly coloured, very noisy and totally mindless on the television. If you'd like to come through to the kitchen, I saved you some food.'

'Oh…but I can't impose on you like that!' she exclaimed infinitely touched by her thoughtfulness. 'It was most kind of you to include Danny, but…'

'An extra mouth or two at the table doesn't make a lot of difference,' she said airily as she led the way down the hallway. 'And please, won't you call me Joyce? Mrs Hennessy is such a mouthful.'

Sam was assailed by a sudden pang of remembrance. There had been a time when *she* had expected to be Mrs Hennessy, too…or rather, *Dr* Hennessy.

She hastily relegated the thought to the back of her mind as her guide paused by one door and pushed it open just a few inches before beckoning Sam forward.

Peering round the edge, she was treated to the sight of three males of assorted ages and sizes sprawled in a heap on a large settee. All three were so intent on the cartoon antics on the screen that they didn't seem to notice that they had an audience themselves.

For one long endless moment Sam's heart was seized by a pang of regret that this wasn't a sight she came home to every night. Danny looked so at home tucked in close on one side of Daniel with his little legs stuck straight out, while Jamie did an impression of a matching bookend on the other side. It looked almost as if they'd been settling down to watch television just like that all their lives.

A gentle hand at her elbow drew her attention away and she took a silent step back into the hallway.

'Let sleeping dogs lie,' her companion murmured as she bustled off again towards the kitchen. 'Time enough to put up with an explosion of noise when you've got some food inside you.'

Spending time in Daniel's home had been the furthest thing from her intention, but Sam couldn't find it in her to object. She had never enjoyed confrontation, and had hated feeling that she was letting people down.

Looking back, she could see that if she'd been able to stand up to her parents she would never have made the disastrous decision to marry Andrew.

Sometimes she wondered how different her life would have been, but then she didn't seem to have changed much over the years if her present predicament was any indication.

Much as she would have liked to scuttle off to the safety of her home with Danny, she found herself being gently bulldozed into a chair and presented with a plate full of something that looked and smelled suspiciously like home-made steak and kidney pudding.

Her stomach growled loudly.

'That's what I like to hear. Unsolicited appreciation before you've even tasted a bite,' Daniel's mother said with a chuckle. 'What would you like with it? Water, juice or tea? I've plenty of all three. If you're anything like Daniel, you don't drink if you're going to be driving, especially with a child in the car.'

'Mrs Hennessy, I'm really very grateful…'

'It's Joyce, remember. And I'm sure you would have taken care of Jamie if the circumstances had been reversed, so none of this gratitude. It really isn't necessary. Now, I know you can't give me any confidential details but did your emergency resolve itself satisfactorily?'

'So far, so good,' Sam said cryptically, knowing she couldn't give a single detail about the events of the last hour or two without compromising the Ashlands' rights. There could hardly be another husband with an amputated hand whose wife was heavily pregnant.

She put the first forkful of food into her mouth and closed her eyes in ecstasy.

'Mmm, this is so good,' she mumbled as the combined flavours of tender meat and succulent gravy wrapped in a perfect suet pastry overwhelmed her taste buds.

'It's only steak and kidney pudding,' Joyce said dismissively. 'Nothing haute cuisine about it.'

'Not all steak and kidney puddings are equal,' Sam pointed out seriously. 'The one and only time I tried to make one of these, the pastry was like leather, the gravy was watery and the meat was as tough as old boots. This is certainly the king of steak and kidney puddings.'

Joyce Hennessy laughed as Sam dived in eagerly for another mouthful. 'It's one of Daniel's favourites, too, and his son's…' Her animation faded slightly when she realised how her words could be taken.

Sam could see that she was feeling uncomfortable and realised that the only solution was to put her cards on the table.

If his mother could accept her explanation of the situation that had arisen over the last five years, perhaps it boded well for Daniel's reaction.

'Has Daniel said anything about knowing me when he was training?' she began, taking the bull by the horns.

'Oh, my dear, he didn't have to. I remember your name well. You were the only colleague he asked me to contact when we were organising Jimmy's funeral.'

Sam was shocked. It wasn't just that the older woman had remembered her name after all this time but the significance of her knowing it in the first place. If only she'd been in a fit state to attend, all her misconceptions would have been straightened out.

The irony was that she'd been so shocked by the supposed death of the man she'd loved that she hadn't been able to go to the one place that would have proved that he was still very much alive.

'My dear, I hope you don't think I'm speaking out of turn, but Daniel was so upset when you didn't come. I think…no, I'm *certain* that he thought you were someone he could count on at such a time. He and Jimmy had always been so close and he was having to shoulder so much on my behalf, and there was no one for him to unburden himself to.'

She was repeatedly tracing the woven pattern around the edge of the tablecloth, her eyes fixed firmly on her task as though she didn't dare glance in Sam's direction.

'It was several weeks before he felt he could leave his father and me with Jamie to visit the hospital. He had to sort out about his leave of absence, but I was almost certain that one of the main reasons why he wanted to go was because he hadn't heard anything from you for such a long time.'

She flicked a single swift glance in her direction and Sam could see an echo of the pain the poor woman must have felt at the time. One son dead and another struggling to cope with the nightmare situation… How much worse had she unwittingly made it?

'He never told me what happened when he spoke to you—in fact he never mentioned your name again until just the other day. All I knew was that he was dreadfully hurt, and absolutely determined that I shouldn't know anything about it.'

'Mrs Hennessy…Joyce,' she corrected herself hurriedly as she pushed her half-finished meal away. How could she enjoy the food when she was filled with so many turbulent emotions? And where on earth did she start to unravel the Gordian knot? All she could do was start at the beginning and hope everything made sense.

'Five years ago I was in love with Daniel and I thought he loved me. When he was called away suddenly to deal with a family emergency he left me a contact number and said he would ring as soon as he could.'

It was difficult, now to remember exactly how many days she'd waited before she'd tried to phone him. Everything had gradually become submerged into the same dark nightmare.

'When I finally got through, there was an elderly woman answering the phone and, when I asked to speak to Dr Hennessy, she told me he was dead.' Sam swallowed and drew in a steadying breath, her shaking fingers laced tightly together on the very edge of the table.

'At that point, all I really knew about Daniel's family was that he had a brother who was working abroad. Perhaps it's because I'm an only child and didn't have much to contribute to family-type conversations. I have no idea why I never realised that they were both doctors. If only I had...'

A comforting hand came to rest over her white-knuckled fists. 'You could waste a whole life if you concentrate on all the might-have-beens,' Joyce said softly. 'I take it he didn't speak to you when he visited the hospital so someone must have told him about your marriage. Did he know you were carrying his child?'

'No, I didn't, but I do now,' said a voice by the door, startling Sam so much that she gave a little shriek and whirled to face him.

'Daniel, don't creep around like that!' his mother chided. 'You'll give me a heart attack!'

'I was coming out to tell you that the two boys are asleep,' he said, his eyes staring unwaveringly at her. 'I can carry Jamie up to bed but I didn't know what to do about Danny.'

The expression on his face told her that there would be no point in trying to deny that Danny was his child. He was obviously in no doubt about her son's parentage.

'If you two will excuse me for a moment,' Joyce Hennessy murmured as she stood up. For a moment, Sam contemplated begging her not to leave but that would be the coward's way.

Daniel barely waited for her tactful departure.

'I didn't know that Danny was my son until his teacher brought him across to introduce him to me,' he said, his voice rough with suppressed emotion. He'd evidently spent the time since he'd made the discovery working up a good head of steam and was ready to explode.

'How could you do that?' he demanded. 'How could you not tell me that you were carrying my son? How could you keep such a thing secret, and then marry another man just weeks later?'

'I didn't know I was pregnant when you left,' she began, but he didn't seem to be listening.

'How many days has it been since you returned to Edenthwaite? How many days since you started working at Denison Memorial? We must have seen each other at least once a day and yet you've never said a word. And how can you justify not telling my mother that she had another grandchild all this time?' he challenged furiously.

Sam felt so guilty.

Granted she had the excuse that she'd thought he was dead but, once she'd come home and discovered that it wasn't true, she should have found some way to tell him. The fact that he had made another woman pregnant just weeks before he'd slept with her didn't alter the fact that he had a right to know that Danny was his child.

She also felt guilty for the degree that she'd once craved parental approval.

She'd been so conscious that she'd let her mother and father down by 'sullying the family name' that she had even agreed to a disastrous marriage to Andrew to legitimise her child.

But Daniel wasn't without blame.

'Wait just a minute,' she protested. 'I know you didn't have any choice about going when your brother asked for help, but you didn't make much effort to keep in touch once you'd gone. If I'd had any idea that you were still alive…' She'd never have dreamed of marrying Andrew, even if Daniel had never proposed, she admitted silently to herself.

'Mum?' said a drowsy voice from the kitchen doorway. 'The video's finished and Jamie's asleep.'

Sam's emotions had still been churning around inside her when she got to bed that night.

It had been relatively easy to get Danny to bed once she'd driven back to the cottage, and the un-accustomed excitement of spending the evening at Daniel's house had worn him out. Within seconds of curling up with his familiar lop-eared rabbit he'd been sound asleep again…but Sam hadn't been so lucky.

As a consequence, today she felt as though she was trying to wade through treacle. The smallest task seemed to be taking forever and, as for the computer glaring balefully at her from the side of her desk…

When one of her patients turned up with a large

painful blood blister under a nail, it was almost a relief to have something totally practical to do.

'I know I could have gone to the accident department over on the other side,' the middle-aged woman confided as Sam scrubbed her hands and donned gloves. 'But I didn't really see the point when I knew they would only call for one of you to come over to see to me. This way, I've got a better chance of choosing who deals with me.'

'Is now the time when I ask you if I was your first choice?' Sam teased, guessing that the chatter was a way of covering up her apprehension.

'Yes and no,' she retorted with a chuckle. 'I said to the receptionist that I didn't mind whether it was you or Dr Hennessy. You, because you're a woman and more likely to be gentle with something to do with hands and nails, and Dr Hennessy because he delivered my first grandchild and wouldn't give up on him until he got him breathing properly. Little tyke is starting to crawl already and into everything, but I would miss him terribly if he hadn't lived...'

'All done!' Sam announced as she straightened up from her task with the last piece of tape holding a protective bandage in place. She was grateful that she wouldn't have to listen to any more paeans of praise for Daniel.

'As I explained, I've bored a little hole through the nail to release the pressure exerted by the collection of blood. By the time the local anaesthetic wears off, the worst of the pain should be gone.'

'Will I lose the nail?' She held her hand up against her shoulder while Sam positioned the temporary sling and tied the knot at the back.

'You might,' Sam warned. 'It's difficult to tell. But

there's a good chance, now, that the nail will eventually grow up normally.'

'I'm just grateful you've taken the pain away. You've got a good touch. Probably comes from having children of your own...' She was still talking as she walked away down the corridor and Sam had to smile.

She was still smiling as she began to tidy away the remaining evidence of her last patient, this time with relief at the knowledge that she had no more patients waiting and would soon be free to find some food.

The smile faded as the woman's words of praise came back.

'Dr Hennessy wouldn't give up on him until he got him breathing properly,' she'd said, and Sam could imagine the scene all too clearly. Daniel had always been very intense when he was working, his concentration complete as he tried to do his best for each patient.

It had always been most noticeable when he was dealing with children and she hadn't needed to be clairvoyant to know that he genuinely liked them.

Unfortunately, that only made her feel more guilty that she hadn't told him about Danny as soon as she'd found out that he hadn't died five years ago. It didn't matter that she had only been one of several. That excuse came from her own feelings of resentment that she hadn't been the love of his life.

What she didn't know, in spite of a long sleepless night, was how to go about remedying the situation.

She could hardly announce to one and all that Daniel was the father of her son. Her own mother would be mortified if the family washing was aired in public like that. But what other reason could she give for Danny spending time with his father—if that was what Daniel decided he wanted?

'But you won't know what he wants to do about the situation until you sit down and talk to him,' she muttered aloud as she carried her bag along the corridor towards their little staff room. 'It's all very well running various scenarios through your head, but...'

'Oh, dear. She's flipped already,' Frankie Long exclaimed from the depths of her chair, a steaming cup of coffee balanced on the flat surface of the wooden arm. 'I know we're a weird lot, but it's happened rather sooner than most. I wonder if you're going to last the whole six months?'

Sam pulled a gruesome face at her and made a beeline for the kettle. She got on well with the thirty-something divorcee, and not just because they were both working single mothers.

At least her own divorce had been relatively amicable. Frankie, on the other hand, had been married to a lawyer and had been forced to fight for every single concession for herself and her two children.

'Sorry,' Frankie murmured when Sam finally collapsed into the neighbouring chair. 'The bitchiness has been let loose with a vengeance this week. Notice how empty the room is? Everyone's found somewhere more congenial to eat.'

'Is there a reason for it, apart from PMT?' Sam asked lightly and startled a chuckle out of her companion.

'That's probably what our male colleagues are thinking but were too terrified to suggest,' Frankie admitted with a groan.

'And?'

'And the answer is something equally hormonal but far less curable,' Frankie said grimly. 'It's the week when my two monsters, who drive me up the wall on a regular basis, are staying with my ex-husband and his new trophy wife.'

'Let me guess. She's half your age with an IQ roughly equal to her bra size,' Sam suggested, having seen the same phenomenon many times during her time in a city hospital. It still amazed her that apparently intelligent men could be totally ruled by their zippers, and never consider the hurt they were doing to their wives and children.

'Got it in one.' Frankie toasted her with the coffee mug. 'Give the girl a prize.'

Sam unwrapped the sandwiches she'd brought with her and took her first bite, then tried to talk through it. 'So, are you depressed because you want him back?'

'Not likely!' Frankie exclaimed. 'She's welcome to him, but I really resent her spending time with my kids.' She tipped her head back against the chair and sighed heavily. 'That's the worst part about the whole situation. Not the infidelity, or the money. The worst part is when the two of them go to stay with their father.'

Sam made an encouraging noise through another large mouthful, savouring the freshly baked bread and thickly sliced, locally cured ham. She'd almost forgotten what the real thing tasted like when you bought it from little local shops rather than the bland pre-packaged variety from supermarkets.

'He never wanted to have much to do with the kids when we were married,' Frankie continued morosely. 'And now he's making this big production about being so caring and concerned. And I'm left at home in the silence of an empty house and I honestly don't know what to do with myself until they come back.'

Now, Sam found herself fighting a shiver. Was that what she would feel like if Daniel insisted on having visitation rights? Would she know what to do with herself for a whole weekend if Danny wasn't home to share it with her?

'How long before they come back?'

'They only went away last night and the weekends are definitely the worst. And, now that you're here, I'm not even on duty so often. I'm going to be reduced to hoping that someone's taken ill just to have something to do.'

'Unless you fancy helping me to do some decorating?' Sam offered impulsively. 'Danny didn't particularly care about the colour of his bedroom until one of the kids at school told him that pink flowered wallpaper was only for girls. He's been badgering me for days and I finally gave in and bought a can of blue paint.'

'Gender stereotyping?' Frankie challenged. 'Actually, I'd love to help, if you mean it. My kids have covered so much of their walls with posters that I can't remember what colour they are. And I certainly wouldn't be allowed to take them down to paint the walls.'

They'd finalised plans for their 'stripping party' and Sam was just enjoying the last few mouthfuls of coffee when Frankie broke the companionable silence.

'You know, my greatest fear is that he'll take them away from me,' she admitted bleakly.

Sam was shocked. 'Do you really think he would?'

'He certainly won't want to have any more…he says two of them are more expense than he needs. But what if trophy-wife wants to play mummy? Will he persuade her that she doesn't need to spoil that fabulous body when she can just take over a ready-made family?'

Sam tried to say something consoling, but the conversation had just gone down an unexpected route and led her to something she hadn't even considered.

Daniel already had his mother available to take care of Jamie when he was at work during the day or called out at night. What if he was to marry? What chance would she, a single working mother, have of keeping her son when there was a place for him with his father and half-brother in a real family?

'Sam. We need to talk,' Daniel announced just as she was getting ready to collect Danny from school.

'Can it wait till tomorrow? Lunch-time, perhaps?' She glanced at her watch and relaxed when she saw that she still had nearly ten minutes in hand. The last thing she wanted was to leave her son standing in the rain waiting for her.

The school staff were unlikely to let that happen, but it was the mental image that drove her to get there on time each day.

'Hardly! That would obviously be too late. I took the liberty of asking my mother to collect Danny at the same time as she gets Jamie,' he announced and completely took her breath away.

'You had absolutely no right to do that!' she exploded, the vague fears that had been plaguing her ever since her conversation with Frankie bursting into their full Technicolor glory. Was this the first step towards taking over her place in her son's life?

He blinked and frowned as though startled by her unexpected vehemence, then his face cleared.

'I take it you haven't had the message, yet?'

'Message? From whom?' Her hands were shaking in spite of the fact that they were tightly clenched round the handle of her bag and her heart was pounding. He couldn't have been to see a solicitor already, could he? She'd always thought legal matters took forever to be decided. And yet he'd said that tomorrow would be too late for their talk…

'Janet Ashland. She's in labour and on her way in and asked specifically for you to be here for the delivery.'

The relief was so great that for a moment she felt quite light-headed.

'So, what did you need to speak to me about in such a hurry? What couldn't wait until tomorrow?' Her emotions had taken her on such a roller-coaster ride that she felt quite sick. A night without much sleep wasn't helping her concentration, either.

'I just thought you would like a few minutes up in the delivery room before Janet arrives,' he said calmly, setting off along the corridor with every expectation that she would meekly follow. 'Hers *is* the first delivery you've done since you started working here, isn't it?'

Now Sam just felt stupid.

If it weren't for her guilty conscience she would never have leapt to such outlandish conclusions when Daniel had merely been trying to help. Her lunchtime conversation with Frankie hadn't helped her level of paranoia in the least.

'Thank you. That would be very helpful,' she agreed weakly. 'Do you know which midwife is on duty?' The midwife would be in charge of the delivery with Sam standing ready in case of serious complications. Hopefully her role would be limited to cheering from the sidelines.

'Faith has been seeing Janet for her regular antenatal visits and will meet us in the delivery room,' Daniel said as he set off up the stairs, his long legs making nothing of the task while she tried vainly to keep up.

That was something that hadn't changed. He *always* forgot that she had shorter legs. The ten-inch difference in their heights had meant that she'd always worn heels when they went out together. Even so, kissing Daniel was something that could be a pain in the neck for both of them…

Kissing Daniel? Where had that come from?

The days when she and Daniel had indulged in kissing were long gone. Even the thought of it was totally inappropriate in the present circumstances.

'They've just arrived at Reception,' Faith announced with a friendly smile, her musical Irish accent sounding quite strange in this part of Cumbria.

'They?' Sam questioned, remembering that Janet's mother had been on standby to accompany her daughter to the hospital.

'Janet and Mark,' she clarified. 'He wasn't going to go into the delivery room with her for fear of passing out. Apparently he's now decided that he can cope with the thought of watching his baby arrive in the world since Janet reminded him exactly how many lambs he's delivered.'

Daniel was still smiling as he took Sam on a rapid

tour of the compact unit, proudly pointing out equipment that wouldn't have looked out of place in a much bigger city hospital.

'So, you see,' he concluded, 'we're ready for almost everything, but we keep our fingers firmly crossed that we won't need to use it.'

'Prepare for the worst and hope for the best?' Sam quoted.

'Exactly so,' Faith agreed, then cocked her head at the sound of approaching voices.

'Oh, wow! Have I got every doctor and nurse in the hospital here?' Janet demanded when she saw the reception committee. Either she had arrived at the hospital wearing a nightdress and dressing gown or had stopped off on the way up to the unit to change. It certainly wasn't one of the hospital's regulation 'no back door' ones, a choice that their expectant mums were allowed to make for themselves.

'Well, what can we say?' Daniel deadpanned. 'It's been a quiet day and this is the only show in town worth watching.'

Sam noticed that Mark was standing quietly in the background looking rather as if he wished he hadn't come, especially as Janet was puffing and blowing her way through another contraction.

'Not quite as informal as lambing, is it, Mark?' she asked as she gave him a hand into the extralarge green gown Faith had found for him. He was so nervous that even with two hands he wouldn't have been in a fit state to manage the ties at the back of his neck.

'You certainly wouldn't be able to afford to eat my lambs if I had to spend this sort of money to bring them into the world,' he said wryly.

'What a good job we're not intending to eat this one, then,' Janet retorted between puffs as she climbed up onto the edge of the bed.

There was a brief pause while Faith took Janet's blood pressure and pulse. 'A little bit raised,' she commented calmly as she slung the stethoscope around her neck and leant forward to help her patient to get comfortable on the bed.

'I'm not surprised,' Janet snapped with unusual sharpness. 'You try clambering around with this much weight strapped around your middle and yours would be a little bit raised, too. We can't all be skinny little whippets.'

Sam couldn't help grinning and narrowly avoided an outright chuckle. If there was one thing Janet would never be, it was a skinny little whippet. She was definitely built on more generous lines that perfectly complemented her big brawny husband.

She caught Daniel's eye and found him fighting laughter, too.

Just that suddenly, they were on the same wavelength, the way they had been right from the first time they'd met.

She'd never forget the way he'd arrived at the last moment for a lecture by a particularly acerbic consultant and, in his haste to find a seat as close as possible to the door in case he was called out, had nearly ended up in Sam's lap.

CHAPTER SEVEN

'I THINK this is more traditional the other way round,' he'd whispered with a wicked gleam in his deep blue eyes. 'Care to try it out sometime?'

Sam was too flustered to reply, overwhelmingly aware of the long lean length of him pressed so tightly against her on the wooden bench. Luckily the lecturer called them all to order and began his presentation, or heaven only knew what gibberish she would have uttered.

As it was, the clever words she'd practised over the next half an hour were never needed. Several times the attentive silence had been broken by the all too familiar sound of a pager and finally, just before the end of the lecture, it was his turn for a shrill summons.

Sam was certain she would remember the wry grin he shot her as he left but she hadn't even seen his name badge to know what he was called. Anyway, she didn't have whatever other women had to have the nerve to search him out.

She had almost been resigned to never seeing him again when there was a knock on the door of her cramped hospital-issue flat.

'So, are you ready to try it?' he'd demanded without preamble as soon as she opened the door, his voice deeper and richer than she'd imagined from a whispered sentence or two in a lecture hall, but his face and body every bit as memorable.

She hadn't forgotten the wicked gleam in those eyes, either, and they were casting the same spell on her unsuspecting senses.

What on earth was wrong with her? She'd never reacted to a man like this before.

In fact, she'd been so intent on her studies, so determined that nothing would deflect her from her eventual goal of becoming a consultant in paediatrics, that she'd barely bothered noticing whether her colleagues were male or female.

Her reaction left her in absolutely no doubt about *him*.

'Ready to try what?' she said breathlessly, hanging on to the edge of the door so that she didn't slide to the floor in a boneless puddle.

'Swapping positions, of course…to see if you prefer sitting on my lap rather than the other way round,' he explained as calmly as if it was the most sensible conversation in the world.

They'd both laughed, and without another word needing to be said he'd stepped into her room and into her life.

It was the laughter in her eyes that had first captivated him, Daniel remembered as he watched the shards of silver gleam in their blue-grey depths.

It had been such a stupid thing to stumble and fall on top of a complete stranger like that, and in front of a room full of professional colleagues it could have been very embarrassing. But then he'd taken one look into those eyes and known she was something special…well worth making a fool of himself.

He'd had to leave the lecture room without finding out her name and it had taken several days to track her down—far longer than he wanted to wait to speak to her again—but there was a little matter of thirty-six hours of almost continuous duty going on at the same time. It hadn't been the first time he'd cursed the intrusion of his pager and it probably wouldn't be the last.

When he'd finally stood outside her door he'd forced himself to pause for several minutes wondering if *this* was the time he made a complete fool of himself.

After all, they'd barely spoken in that lecture theatre. They'd sat side by side for nearly an hour but he had no way of knowing if she'd been as totally aware of the heat their bodies seemed to generate everywhere they touched.

For all he knew she was already in a committed relationship, a woman as beautiful as she was...

He straightened his shoulders and drew in a steadying breath, still not certain why this woman among all the others he'd met should seem so important.

In the end, the only way to find out was to lift his hand up and knock.

Then she'd opened the door and he'd met her eyes again and he knew.

All he could think was that it had been like coming home at the end of a long journey.

From that moment there had been no more questions in his mind. Everything had been easy...effortless...sublime...right up until he had that phone call from his brother.

That was the moment when everything fell apart.

After that phone call, nothing had been the same.

Within weeks, the life he'd planned with such growing certainty had changed forever.

Not only had he lost a treasured older brother but he'd lost the woman he loved and taken on the responsibility of raising a motherless child.

For a long time he'd railed against Fate but he'd never thought she had a sense of humour.

Never for an instant had he contemplated the possibility that Sam would divorce, or that they would end up working in the same part of the country, let alone in the same medical centre. He'd certainly never envisioned finding out that in that brief perfect time they'd had together he'd given her a child.

But somehow, the most startling discovery of all was the fact that, after everything that had happened in the last five years, they still shared the same sense of humour and could communicate with nothing more than a fleeting glance.

Was there some mysterious significance to that, or was it just another cosmic joke being played at his expense?

A strangled groan snatched him out of his musings in time to witness the new baby's head emerging.

'You certainly didn't arrive with much time to spare,' Faith commented as she ran practised fingers around the baby's neck to check that the cord wasn't wrapped around it.

'Don't have much time to waste on a farm,' Janet said through gritted teeth, one hand tightly clasping her husband's meaty paw. '*Please*, can I push again? *Now!*'

'As soon as you like, darlin' girl,' Faith invited with a chuckle. 'All's clear at this end and I can't wait to see whether this is a girl or a boy.'

'It won't matter either way,' Mark said firmly with a smile and a pointed look in Sam's direction. 'Girl or boy, we've decided it's going to be called Sam because, if it weren't for her, I wouldn't be here to see it born.'

Daniel didn't have time to ponder the heartfelt statement because at that point baby Ashland arrived in the world and immediately began complaining.

'How about celebrating your namesake's arrival with a cup of coffee?' Daniel suggested when they finally left the maternity unit.

Sam glanced at her watch and blinked in surprise.

'I didn't realise what the time was,' she exclaimed. 'The labour was perfectly normal and straightforward and was over so quickly that I thought we'd only been here an hour. It's long past time that I collected Danny.'

'It was the arrival of the family that took the time. They all wanted to meet you, especially as their newest member was named after you,' he pointed out. 'Anyway, there's no problem over Danny. I phoned my mother while you were getting your things. She told me that they finally flaked out in front of *The Jungle Book* half an hour ago so she's put them to bed.'

'What, both of them?' Sam frowned, not completely sure how she felt about that. She certainly trusted Joyce to be able to look after her precious son. She had a feeling that she had already accepted him as if he had always been part of the family.

'Jamie has got plenty of spare clothes and there's a bunk bed in his room so that he can have visitors to stay for the night. Rather than drag Danny out of bed, you could collect him after breakfast in the morning. It is Saturday, after all. So—' he returned to his original question '—knowing that Danny isn't waiting anxiously for you to arrive, do you want a cup of coffee?'

It was hours since she'd last had anything to drink and even longer since that sandwich at lunch-time. Just the thought of food made her stomach rumble…loudly.

He couldn't avoid hearing it.

'Hmm,' he said with a grin. 'How about making that a celebratory meal? They do some fairly substantial bar snacks at the White Hart, or there's Roberto's if you prefer Italian, or the Chinese takeaway.'

Sam knew she shouldn't accept, not when there were so many things still undecided between the two of them, but the offer was irresistible. Especially when she was this hungry.

'I'm not really dressed up enough for Roberto's—' she gestured towards her perfectly serviceable skirt and blouse, the jacket folded over one arm '—and as for Chinese takeaway…'

'You're always starving hungry again half an hour later and need to order another one,' he chimed in with a chuckle.

She was surprised that he'd remembered something so stupid after all this time, but it set off a warm glow somewhere deep inside. Unfortunately, the rest of her insides were determined to let her know that they wanted to be filled. Now.

'So it looks as if it's the White Hart, then, by default,' she said brightly, trying to cover up the unexpected shiver of excitement that insisted on making itself felt at the idea of spending time with Daniel. 'I wonder if they're still using the same menus as when I last went there? I don't think they'd changed in about ten years, even then.'

'Is that the place you tried to order soup in a basket?' he asked, proving once again that he'd remembered things she'd told him all that time ago.

'And the waitress didn't even crack a smile. Just patiently explained that they didn't have that on the menu and would I prefer chicken or scampi?' Sam finished. 'Yes, that's the one. Although, to be fair, their meals might be limited but the quality is so good that they really don't need to change the menus. I suppose it was just a symptom of the fact that I was ready to move away from home and try my wings that the sameness was getting to me.'

They'd reached the staff car park behind the GP unit by this time and Sam automatically unlocked her little compact and climbed in, depositing her bag on the seat beside her.

'I'll see you at the White Hart, Sam,' Daniel called as his own car chirped in response to the electronic fob. 'Don't forget to lock your bag out of sight in the boot before you leave the car. Even in idyllic places like Edenthwaite drugs are becoming a problem.'

Sam was glad of the reminder. Her brain was so scrambled that she would probably have forgotten her own name without prompting.

Considering it was Friday night, they were lucky to get one of the few tables with any privacy, but Sam was quite certain that it wouldn't have mattered if they had been sitting in the middle of a spotlight.

After several weeks of stilted communication and the odd startling revelation, it seemed as if they were at last starting to find the same wavelength. Perhaps the barriers had finally been breached by the shared experience of watching baby Sam's arrival into the world.

Whatever the reason, their conversation ranged far and wide as they devoured their servings of scampi and chips, then shared an extra order of chips.

'I'm going to regret this when I get on the scales in the morning,' Sam groaned. 'I've been trying to lose those last few pounds ever since Danny was born.'

'I can't see why you'd bother,' he said in a husky voice after a brief but loaded silence. He treated her to a slow glance that left her tingling with awareness. 'I can't see anything that would look better if it was smaller.'

'Daniel!' she muttered as heat flushed her cheeks, embarrassed but definitely delighted with the compliment. 'I think that last glass of orange juice must have gone to your head.'

He shook his head, his eyes growing darker as the expression in them became more heated. 'You were beautiful five years ago but now you're somehow more...more ripe...more womanly...if that word isn't a hanging offence these days.'

The tingling awareness that had begun with his admiring gaze had grown with each word. Deep inside she felt the hard cold wall of ice around her heart begin to melt and the emotions she'd tried to deny for so long warmed her like the first rays of sunshine after a bitter winter.

'Can I get you anything else?' enquired the cheer-

ful voice of their attentive waitress. 'A coffee, perhaps? Or a dessert? Would you like to see the menu
again?'

The growing intensity of the moment was shattered and the mention of the infamous menu was
enough to make them both smile.

'Just the bill, please,' Daniel said and while Sam
realised that this had been a pleasant interlude, there
was no logic to the disappointment she was feeling.

Anyway, the evening had to end some time. They
could hardly sit and talk all night or they would become the focus of talk themselves.

'Drive carefully,' he warned, in spite of the fact
that both of them had chosen to stick to soft drinks.
They certainly hadn't needed any alcohol to make
the evening enjoyable. 'I'll follow you to make sure
you get home safely.'

'There's no need to do that,' she said, amazed to
realise how his concern warmed her and made her
feel cherished. 'I might not have passed my test very
long ago but I've had a lot more practice since I
came home to Edenthwaite than I would have if I'd
stayed in the city.'

'Even so, I'll follow you home,' he insisted quietly
and closed her door.

She was very conscious that the lights following
her along the road to her cottage belonged to Daniel
but when she drew into her driveway she was surprised to see them follow her through the stone built
gateposts and park right behind her.

'Is there a problem?' she asked when they met
halfway between the two cars. 'I was expecting you
to turn and go back home.'

'No problem, except I couldn't wait any longer,'

he said in a low growl as he framed her face between his hands and tilted his head towards her.

The first brief contact between their lips was almost tentative, as if he wasn't sure how she would react.

That wasn't true of the second encounter. This time he couldn't help knowing that she wanted the kiss every bit as much as he did as she tilted her head and parted her lips eagerly to welcome him in.

Sam couldn't believe just how familiar he tasted and felt after all this time. The connection between them was so strong that it was almost as if it had been just hours or days since their last embrace and yet she'd missed him so much that it could have been an eternity since she'd felt his arms around her.

'Ah, Sam, I've missed you,' he groaned when he came up briefly to snatch a lungful of air.

She didn't have a chance to echo his words as he brought his mouth to meet hers and took her straight down into the depths of passion again.

Time ceased to have any real meaning as arousal took over and it was only the jangle as her keys hit the ground that allowed reality to intrude.

'I can't believe we're doing this,' he muttered as he grasped each of her shoulders in one broad palm. Sam wasn't certain whether he was holding on to her to keep the two of them apart or because he knew that she wasn't capable of standing up alone.

'Doing what?' she murmured, wishing there was more light so that she could see the effect their kisses was having on him.

She'd always been fascinated to see the way his eyelids grew heavy when his pupils dilated with arousal, and the way his lips became fuller and darker as their kisses caused the sensitive tissues to become engorged.

'We're standing out here necking like a couple of teenagers,' he pointed out in exasperation as he crouched down to search for her keys. 'At our age!'

'And don't forget your height,' she groaned, giving her neck a rub. She'd almost forgotten that there could be serious disadvantages to this kissing game. A stiff neck was just one of them.

He straightened up with the missing keys and held them out to her but didn't release them when she held out her hand.

'Sam,' he said softly, his words reaching her clearly through the still evening air. 'Are you going to invite me in?'

She should have said no.

Every cautious, rational cell in her body was screaming at her as she led the way up to her bedroom, but her heart knew what it wanted.

And what it wanted was Daniel.

He'd offered no guarantees and made no promises and for all she knew this was going to be just a one-night stand but for the first time in her life she didn't care.

She'd loved him from the moment she first met him and had never ceased to mourn him when she believed he'd died. To have him here, now, was more than she had ever dreamed.

How many times over those first desperate weeks had she wept for just one more chance to hold him in her arms?

How many times in the long years since had she felt guilty that she was unable to respond to any other man the way she had to him, not even Andrew, her husband?

How often had she tried to remember every turn and move he'd made as he took his clothes off? The way the soft lamplight gilded his skin and outlined the shape and movement of each bone and muscle as he began to remove her clothes, too.

For the sake of her sanity she'd had to try to forget the careful way he used to position the two of them on her narrow single bed, supporting his weight so that he didn't overwhelm her slighter frame.

She'd never been able to forget.

All she had to do was see him reach for the knot in his tie to know exactly the way he would pull until one end slid completely out. Next came his shirt, each button meticulously unfastened while his eyes continued to devour her from head to foot.

Her heart was pounding loud enough to echo off the walls by the time he stepped out of his trousers and reached for the waistband of his dark blue underwear.

His shoulders were broader, she thought as he walked towards her, casting her into shadow as he stepped between her and the bedside light.

'Far too many buttons,' he whispered as he painstakingly attended to each one. Was it her faulty imagination or were those steady-as-a-rock surgeon's hands trembling? Was his breathing as uneven as hers and his heart racing? Was he on fire with anticipation, too, desperate for that first contact of skin on skin?

And then, finally, they were both naked and in her bed and he wrapped his arms around her.

She wanted to savour every second and make it

last but the feel of his body against hers was like throwing a match on tinder.

Suddenly she couldn't be close enough, hold him tight enough, kiss him long enough, couldn't wait another second before they ceased to be two separate people and joined together as one.

Sam woke to the sound of the dawn chorus as light began to creep round the edges of the curtains and her heart sank.

Her once-in-a-lifetime night was nearly over.

It had been more and better than anything she could have imagined, and Daniel had been the caring passionate sensual insatiable lover of every woman's dreams.

Now all she had to do was find a way to keep her dignity until Daniel went on his way.

She'd been so certain that she wouldn't regret what they'd done but she'd been wrong. She already regretted the fact that this wasn't ever going to happen again. How could it in a place like Edenthwaite? As it was, she wouldn't be at all surprised if her arrival at work was greeted with knowing smiles.

In such close-knit communities news and rumours flew with equal speed and their cosy meal at the White Hart had probably already set tongues wagging. If the owners of those tongues were to even suspect that Dr Daniel Hennessy had spent the night with Dr Denison's daughter, she'd never hear the end of it.

Especially from her mother.

Sam nearly groaned aloud at the thought of what *that* pillar of the community would have to say.

She turned her head just far enough to be able to

catch a glimpse of Daniel sleeping and met a pair of darkly knowing eyes.

'Hello, beautiful,' he murmured, his early-morning rusty voice sending shivers up her spine as he reached for her. 'You're too far away.'

Sam chuckled as she found her familiar niche with her head tucked under his chin and her ear pressed over his heart, their arms wrapped around each other.

'Too far away in a single bed?' she teased and breathed in the familiar mixture of soap and skin and the natural musk of an aroused male that would always mean 'Daniel' to her.

'Regrets?' he asked softly when she grew still.

'No,' she answered honestly, because how could she have regrets when she was lying here with him? 'But several second thoughts and even third thoughts about the sense of what we've done.'

It had been at least halfway through the night before she'd realised that neither of them had thought about taking any precautions against pregnancy. By that time they'd already made love so often that a few more times weren't going to make much difference. After he had gone she was going to have to consult her private diary before she would know whether history was going to repeat itself.

The thought of carrying another of Daniel's babies sent a pang of longing through her. Danny was a lovely boy full of life and love and mischief and she would love the chance to have another.

How many times since Danny was born had she wished that Daniel was alive to see him? She had longed in vain to share his antics and achievements with the father who had given him to her. If she were pregnant now...

'Be careful what you wish for,' she murmured under her breath. They still hadn't spoken about the fact that Daniel was Danny's father, yet. How could she possibly be contemplating another child?

Because she loved him, was the simple answer that came to her as the man in question began to seduce her once again, in spite of the time showing on her alarm clock.

There really wasn't time for this if they were going to keep their overnight tryst secret from the rest of the town, but when he leant over her and took her mouth with his there was no way she could refuse him.

'I just feel so tired all the time,' Jason Caddick complained wearily as he slumped in the chair beside Sam's desk.

That makes two of us, she thought wryly, but at least I know what caused mine and he's sitting just a few yards away through that wall.

She firmly switched her concentration back to the young man in front of her, the elder of Peter Caddick's three children at seventeen.

'Have you mentioned this to your father?' she probed gently, not wanting to end up in the middle of some sort of family problem.

'A while ago when I was doing a lot of sport training,' he admitted. 'I was also doing extra study for my school exams and he said I was just overdoing it a bit and to give my body a chance.'

'And?'

'I got so tired that I had to give up all my training and even then it hasn't got any better.'

'Any other problems?' she took his wrist and

found that he was rather warm and his pulse was far too rapid for a fit young man. There were several bruises on his arms, clearly visible below the loose sleeves of his T-shirt, and the insides of his lower eyelids were far too pale, too.

'I've been getting a bit short of breath when I take the dog out for a walk or play football in the garden with my brother. And my joints have been aching,' he offered hesitantly then gave an embarrassed laugh. 'I sound like an old crock, don't I? At least ninety.'

'Not at all,' she reassured him. 'They're called symptoms for a reason. The word also means sign, indication and warning.'

'Well, all the indications, signs and warnings are that I'm falling apart. *And* I'm probably going to end up without any teeth if my gums keep bleeding the way they are. I'll have to visit the dentist, next, for dentures.'

The little warning bell that had been sounding in the distance had suddenly turned into a siren at close quarters.

'Well, Jason, as you probably know from having a GP as a father, one way of weeding out the real symptoms from the also-rans is to do some basic tests. Unfortunately, it's legally classed as an assault if I try to take a blood sample from you without permission and, until you're eighteen, that means I'll have to ask one of your parents…'

'Not any more,' he interrupted in a hurry. 'If you look at my file you'll see that, as of today, I can sign myself over to Dracula any time I like.' He glanced away for a moment before meeting her gaze again. 'I hope you don't mind me doing it this way, but that's why I deliberately made the appointment with you for today. Dad's not on duty this morning and Mum's too busy flapping around about my party to notice that I've sloped off. I wasn't strictly truthful with the receptionist here, either. She thinks I'm in here inviting you to my party.'

'Well, at least we can keep our stories straight,' she said, understanding only too well what an awkward situation he found himself in. Perhaps the fact that she had once been in the same position with her father a GP in the same practice was the reason why he'd chosen to see her.

'Now, how about celebrating your coming of age with me taking a couple of samples of blood?' she suggested as she pulled out some forms. 'On *my* eighteenth I decided to travel all the way to Keighley just to donate a unit of blood for the first time. Far more worthwhile than going out to a pub and getting legless. Unfortunately, I hadn't realised that I should rest for a while afterwards and nearly ended up arriving home late for my party.'

She kept up the neutral chatter while she filled the requisite containers, then sent him off to produce a urine specimen to complete the set.

'We should have the results back on those in a couple of days,' she said with a reassuring smile when she'd completed the paperwork. 'In the meantime, I hope you have a great party.'

He already had his hand on the doorknob when he stopped and looked back at her.

'You won't say anything about this to Dad?' he said with sudden urgency. 'I mean, if it's just anaemia or something simple like an infection I could take a course of tablets without them ever knowing.'

That placed Sam firmly in a cleft stick.

'You're probably well aware that now you've reached eighteen it isn't legal for me to break patient confidentiality, Jason, but what if—God forbid—the results come back with something more serious? Don't you think you ought to confide in your parents so that they can give you their support?'

He leant his head wearily back against the door, looking less and less like a young man on the threshold of adulthood. At the moment he just seemed very scared and uncertain and as if he needed a consoling hug.

'Can we make a pact?' she suggested. 'I'll keep quiet until the results come through but then I'll leave it to you to tell your parents what you've been up to…unless you decide you'd like me to do it for you.'

His wry smile was a pretty good approximation of one she'd seen on his father's face. 'Dad said the other day that you drive a hard bargain and I can see what he means. You're determined that I'm going to be adult about this whether I want to or not.'

'Welcome to the real world,' she said with an ironic grimace, then deliberately lightened the mood. 'Just promise me that you won't tell my son what I'm really like. He still thinks I'm wonderful.'

Several hours later she would have been forced to eat her words.

Danny didn't often succumb to bad temper but this evening he was really playing up.

'I don't *want* to have a bath. It's too early,' he shouted as he made a beeline for his bedroom with tears streaming down his little face. 'I want to go to Jamie's house and play. Jamie's house is much better. It's bigger and he's got lots of videos of cartoons.'

'But, Danny, *this* is your house until we find a new one, and it's time for your bath,' she repeated persuasively. 'Jamie won't be playing, now, either. He'll be getting ready for bed, too. Anyway, you need to get to sleep soon or you won't be awake by the time we're ready to paint the yukky flowery walls. Remember, Dr Frankie is coming to help?'

She sighed when he didn't reply, his face buried in his pillow and a stranglehold on his favourite toy for comfort. She couldn't really blame him for wanting to spend time with his friend, and tonight's tantrum was probably partly the result of too much excitement and too little sleep.

'Do you want me to draw the bath water for you tonight?' she suggested slyly, knowing how jealously he guarded the newly acquired right.

'No!' he exclaimed instantly, bouncing up to stare at her indignantly. '*I* do my water,' and he slid off the bed to hurry out of the room.

She perched gratefully on the edge of the bed while she followed the sound of his feet going through her bedroom and into the bathroom. Next there was the sound of water gushing into the bath, closely followed by the rhythmic thump, thump that told her he was bouncing on her bed.

'Don't forget to turn the taps off,' she reminded him from the top of the stairs a couple of minutes later and waited until she heard his feet hit the floor and hurry to do her bidding.

At least it looked as if the bad temper was forgotten for the moment, she thought as she made her way down to check on the supper. She had more than enough to think about with the results that had come through from the labs just before she left the surgery.

'Poor Jason,' she sighed, wondering how he was going to take the news that he had leukaemia. What would it do to his plans to go to medical school? Would he be fit enough to take the important exams to secure his place and if he passed them, would he be well enough to begin the course?

It went against the grain to keep a diagnosis to herself, especially such a life-threatening one, but she couldn't break the news to Jason tonight, knowing that his eighteenth birthday party was due to start at any moment.

The only good part about the results was that his initial white blood cell count was on the low side; that, and the fact that the first intensive course of chemotherapy brought more than ninety per cent of children with acute lymphocytic leukaemia into remission.

She wouldn't allow herself to dwell on the possibility that Jason's treatment could be anything but successful.

CHAPTER EIGHT

'SO, MY friend. What's got you so down in the mouth today?' Frankie challenged from the top of the ladder as she scraped at a particularly stubborn strip of wallpaper.

Sam glanced behind her and discovered that Danny had apparently grown bored with his task of stuffing soggy paper into black plastic bags. It obviously wasn't nearly as interesting as having permission to pull the much-hated pink flowers off the walls.

'Just worried about a patient,' she said guardedly. 'Eighteen years old and diagnosed with ALL.'

'Ouch!' Frankie grimaced. 'It's bad enough when it's the under-tens because we know their recovery rate from acute lymphocytic leukaemia is so good now. Unfortunately, the closer they get to twenty...'

She didn't need to complete the thought. Sam had looked the statistics up after Danny had gone to bed last night. The treatment Jason could expect to undergo had made depressing reading, too. He could be looking at up to three years of it, depending on how successful the first round of intensive chemotherapy was. And that was if he *did* go into remission. The alternative was unthinkable.

'A family friend?' Frankie probed gently when she realised that Sam was still preoccupied, tacitly offering a listening ear in the way Sam would if the positions were reversed. 'Someone I would know?'

'Son of a friend,' Sam corrected obliquely to put her off the track and left it at that. Being GPs in the same practice, it was quite in order for them to discuss patients, as any one of them might be called out in an emergency. In this case, she wasn't going to say anything until she'd had a chance to break the news to Jason and his parents.

Once they knew, she hadn't a doubt that Peter would say something to the rest of his colleagues. That was one thing she'd noticed when Grace Potter had been forced to take early maternity leave—the way the rest of her colleagues pulled together to support her. She hadn't a doubt that the same thing would happen with the Caddick family.

This day-to-day camaraderie was deeper than the surface friendships she'd known over the last five years. It was something that she'd missed during her time in big city hospitals, and one of the reasons why she was hoping that her temporary post at Denison Memorial had a chance of becoming permanent.

'Mummy! Mummy!' Danny shrieked from outside the cottage and Sam's heart leapt into her throat. She was on her way down the stairs almost before she realised that her feet were moving.

Danny's high-pitched voice was still calling her as she burst out into the garden and found Daniel at the front gate.

'Mummy! Jamie's here!' he squealed excitedly. 'He says I can go and play at his house.'

Sam pressed a shaky hand over her pounding heart and waited for it to resume its usual place in her chest. She'd been so certain that her precious son was shrieking because he was hurt that she felt quite shaky.

'Sam? Are you all right? You look very pale,' Daniel said, his voice almost drowned out by Danny's insistent demand.

'Can I go now, Mummy? I want to play with Jamie's cars. And watch a video. Can I?'

'Hush a minute, Danny. There's something wrong with your mother,' Daniel said quietly and the child subsided instantly.

'There's nothing wrong. Really,' she insisted when he looked doubtful. 'It's just that when I heard Danny shouting like that I thought he'd been injured.'

'And you raced out here expecting to see severed limbs and oceans of gore,' he added with an understanding smile. 'And instead you find us here to invite the two of you to join us for the day.'

'Oh, Daniel, we can't,' she said with a gesture towards her scruffy glue-splattered jeans and shapeless T-shirt.

'How long would it take you to change? We're quite happy to wait.'

The two boys were listening to the conversation with their heads going backwards and forwards like spectators at a tennis match. They were already jumping up and down with excitement.

'We were decorating Danny's bedroom,' Sam began when another voice chimed in from the open bedroom window.

'And if you think you're taking them away and leaving me to do all the hard work, Daniel Hennessy, you've got another think coming!'

For one awful moment Sam actually resented Frankie for being there.

Her heart had leapt for an entirely different reason

when she'd seen him standing at her gate and, as for the invitation to spend the day with him...

But she'd enlisted Frankie's help and was now honour-bound to finish the job.

'Danny could go to keep Jamie company,' she suggested, much to the boys' delight. 'But he'd have to come back at a reasonable time to go to bed because there's school in the morning.'

Permission granted, the two boys hurried to let themselves into Daniel's car, chattering nineteen to the dozen all the way.

Daniel paused just long enough to murmur mournfully, 'But this means there's no one to keep *me* company.'

His deep blue eyes were still gleaming wickedly when he waved a cheery hand in Frankie's direction and went to fold his long length into the car.

She was still trying to subdue her reaction to the suggestive tone of his words when she rejoined Frankie in Danny's bedroom.

'He's Danny's father, isn't he?' Frankie said without a scrap of hesitation, speculation clear in her eyes. 'Those boys are like two peas in a pod, and each a perfect miniature of their father.'

Sam nodded mutely. She had been dreading this moment for so long that it was almost a relief to have it happen at last.

'He does know, doesn't he?' Frankie's forehead was pleated into a frown. She was obviously having trouble working out the logistics of two children so close in age, as would everybody else who saw them together.

'He does *now*.'

Sam sighed and perched one hip on the edge of

the windowsill. She might as well get used to this. Edenthwaite residents were not backwards about coming forwards and she was probably going to have to give the edited version of past events several times before the gossips managed to spread it to all and sundry.

At least her own version would be on nodding acquaintance with the truth.

'You mean, until Daniel walked into the staff room on your first morning at Denison Memorial you believed he was *dead*?' Frankie was clearly astounded. 'The air between you was so thick that I knew I was picking up on something, but I thought it was a case of love at first sight...or at least a dose of good healthy lust.'

Sam felt the wash of heat spread up over her cheeks and Frankie hooted.

'Ah ha! The plot thickens!' she exclaimed gleefully. 'So you *do* still want to do the wild thing with him!'

'Frankie!' She must be scarlet by now. Wild was a very good word for the way they had been together, and, yes, she *did* want to do it again.

'Silly question! Of course you do,' Frankie answered herself. 'He's hard working, good at his job, nice to children and old ladies and good-looking enough to be the next James Bond. Why *wouldn't* you want to drag him into your bed?'

'Why indeed?' Sam said dryly, knowing Daniel was all those things and more.

Their night together had proved beyond doubt that the attraction between them was as strong as ever, but they could hardly embark on a wild affair while living in Edenthwaite. Such 'big city' behaviour would be totally unacceptable, especially to the people in her mother's circle, and there was no way she would make her son the target of the gossips' tongues.

Anyway, she still hadn't had that all-important conversation with Daniel, yet. As the old-fashioned expression went, she had no idea what his intentions were. She didn't even know if *she* was ready to embark on the uncertainty of a long-term relationship. She'd already failed once.

And then there was Danny to think about.

Judging from his reaction just a few minutes ago, he would undoubtedly benefit from having his father in his life. But what if the relationship between Daniel and herself disintegrated? Would that cause him more pain than if he'd never found out who his father was?

'Hello, in there? Anybody home?' Frankie teased as she clicked her fingers right in front of Sam. 'I'm obviously not going to be able to get anything sensible out of you so we might as well get on with the work.'

She stood up from her perch on the bottom step of the ladder and stretched her arms above her head as though limbering up for a session of aerobics, then paused.

'Just… If you want a word of unsolicited advice, take it slowly,' she said diffidently, as though not certain she should be speaking at all. 'My ex and I went into things too hot and heavy and by the time they cooled down there were two boys caught in the middle. You've already got one and so has he, and the fact that they're already related is no guarantee that things will work out.'

'Don't worry about that,' Sam agreed fervently. 'Something permanent isn't even on the cards, yet, so you can be certain I'm not going to go racing up to Gretna Green at the first opportunity.'

The rest of the morning was spent discussing a variety of lighter topics with their hands working just as fast as their tongues.

Sam had prepared sandwiches for lunch and had intended reheating a couple of cartons of home-made lasagne for their evening meal.

'Not for me,' Frankie said as they stood in the bedroom doorway admiring the fruits of their labours. 'I'm going straight home to wallow up to my neck in a bath full of expensively scented water with that new Debussy CD playing just for me. There's half a bottle of white wine in the fridge and I've got a very quick recipe for spaghetti carbonara that I'll share with you some time.'

'But you've worked so hard. I feel guilty that all I gave you for lunch was some sandwiches.'

'Sam, you helped me get through another lonely day without my kids without going into a depression and that was worth more that I can tell you. If you insist, I shall get you to come and do some ghastly menial job at my place one day.'

Sam waved as Frankie drove away and went back up to have a last look at Danny's revamped bedroom.

The hated pink flowers and pale pink ceiling were gone forever, replaced by Wedgwood blue painted walls and a white ceiling. Luckily the woodwork was already white and hadn't needed changing so there wasn't the smell of oil-based paint to contend with.

'Almost as good as one of those television make-over programmes,' she murmured as she propped the door open to make sure that everything was dry and aired by the time Danny returned.

She ran her fingers through her hair and grimaced when she felt the dried blobs of paint sticking the strands together.

'Frankie had the right idea,' she decided as she made for the bathroom. 'A long hot bath with a dollop of perfume in it sounds just right.'

Soon she was up to her neck in scented water. Her hair was so clean it squeaked when she ran her fingers through it and every bone and muscle was about to dissolve. It felt wonderful. So mindless and relaxing that if she wasn't careful she could be in danger of falling asleep...

'Sam?' called a familiar male voice somewhere in the distance and she smiled lazily.

There was no need to open her eyes because she knew who it was. Daniel spent a lot of time in her thoughts and in her dreams these days. The only pity was that she didn't know if he was going to be in her life.

He'd said that he'd never been married, but he'd never mentioned Jamie's mother. Was the woman still part of his life? Was she the reason why Daniel had never married?

'Sam? Where are you...?'

Daniel's voice stopped abruptly but it had been so close and so real this time that she opened her eyes and found him standing in the doorway.

'Sam,' he breathed, his gaze riveted on the sight that met him in the tiny bathroom. She was like some pagan water nymph as she lay there in the bath.

Should he have apologised and left the room? It

wasn't an option. The only direction his feet wanted to go was towards her as he tried to devour her with his eyes.

She was looking up at him almost as if she'd expected him to find her like this, making no attempt to cover herself as she gazed up out of liquid blue-grey eyes.

'Did you find Mummy?' demanded a piercing treble voice and they both jerked in shock at the unexpected intrusion of the rest of the world.

Before Daniel could get himself together to make a strategic retreat Danny was there beside him apparently so enthralled with his room that he was totally unconcerned by the proprieties.

'Mummy, did you see my bedroom?' he exclaimed, clearly delighted. 'There's no yukky flowers any more. It's really great. Can I have bunk beds so Jamie can come and stay? There's nowhere for him to sleep…unless we share *my* bed.'

He whirled and ran back through Sam's bedroom without waiting for a reply.

Daniel couldn't help the chuckle that escaped him as he reached for a towel.

'I love them at this age. They've got such one-track minds.'

Sam snorted. She was juggling with the towel as she stood up, apparently trying to wrap it around herself without dipping the ends in the water—although why she was bothering to contort herself like that he didn't know. It wasn't as if he hadn't already seen everything she had to show, and approved of every inch. She hadn't been concerned with hiding herself when she'd been lying in the bath.

'All men have one-track minds, Daniel. It's a neurological fact,' she quipped with a cheeky grin. 'Anyway, thank God for it, otherwise we'd be standing here trying to explain…' She gestured wordlessly between the two of them and their surroundings.

Daniel suppressed a pang of regret that there hadn't been something more between them than just a few seconds of silent appreciation, but he was certain that even a single-minded five-year-old would have noticed his mother being seduced in the bath.

'I'd better leave you in peace and take Jamie back home,' he suggested. Not that he wanted to leave her like this. His body was clamouring to do far more than merely look at her and, as far as her feelings were concerned, just the expression in her eyes had told him more than he'd expected to learn.

Perhaps there was a chance that the two of them could take up where they'd left off five years ago. Perhaps happily ever after really was a possibility.

'Has my last patient arrived?' Sam asked, dreading the moment.

'About three minutes ago. I took him straight through to the nurses' room as you asked,' Anne Townsend reported, clearly intrigued by the cloak-and-dagger antics.

It was a good job that Sam knew the senior receptionist was utterly trustworthy when it came to patient confidentiality. She was walking a very fine line this morning and wasn't enjoying it one bit. If Peter Caddick emerged from his room at the wrong moment and realised that his son was waiting to consult one of his colleagues rather than his own father, he would probably be very hurt.

What he was going to feel when he found out the

diagnosis she had made didn't bear thinking about. Sam had spent some time over the weekend wondering how she would feel if it were happening to Danny and realised it was beyond imagination.

'Dr Sam,' Jason said as he stood politely to offer her his hand. 'Thanks for organising all this. I know it must have put you in a difficult situation, especially as you're new here.'

'Nonsense, Jason,' she said dismissively as she gestured for him to sit again. 'I'm just glad that you felt you could come to me.'

'So, what's the verdict, doc? Am I pregnant?' he joked, but in spite of the humour Sam could see that he was uneasy.

'I can almost guarantee that you aren't going to have to worry about getting pregnant,' she retorted, then had to drop the light-hearted banter while she tried to break the news gently. 'Jason, I'm sorry but I *did* find a problem in your tests. A problem with your blood.'

'More serious than simple anaemia?' he prompted, the expression in his eyes suddenly far older than his age. 'As serious as leukaemia?'

Sam should have realised that such an intelligent boy might have worked it out for himself; especially one with a GP for a father.

She nodded. 'ALL,' she elaborated quietly.

He heaved a shaky sigh. 'So…that means an immediate blasting with heavy-duty chemo to try to get me into remission, then, if it's successful, follow-up sessions over the next two or three years to be certain it's been knocked on the head.'

He'd managed to keep going right to the end even though his voice had cracked under the strain.

Sam reached for one of his tightly clenched hands and pressed it between hers. 'Are you ready to tell your dad now, Jason?' she asked quietly. 'I could bring him in here without anyone else knowing and let you do it in your own way, or I could be here with you if you feel you want a bit of support.'

'I shouldn't need anyone's support. He's my *dad*,' he exclaimed with a troubled expression.

'Except you're going through a transitional time at the moment. You're still living at home and going to school and yet you're old enough to vote, get married, make all sorts of major decisions that will affect the whole of your life. It's only natural that you're still trying to work out what these changes are having on your relationship with your parents.'

'You make it sound so simple and logical,' he complained.

'When real life is anything but simple and logical,' she said with an understanding squeeze. 'It's all emotions and attitudes and redrawing of boundaries.'

He was silent for a long moment before he straightened his shoulders.

'Would you go and get my dad now?' he asked quietly. 'I'd like you to stay for the first few minutes when he gets here but then...'

'I know how to fade into the wallpaper,' she promised and left the room full of admiration for a very courageous young man.

'Sam, we've got a problem over in the Domino unit,' Daniel told her, his deep voice sending its usual shiver down her spine even down the telephone.

'Anything I can do?' she offered immediately. 'Always bearing in mind that it's my turn to collect the boys from school.'

That was one difference their growing rapport had brought. There was very rarely a scramble at the end of the school day these days now that they were combining the load and sharing the journeys. Jamie and Danny thoroughly approved of the new arrangement because they got to play together until the visitor was collected and taken home.

The fact that it meant that Sam and Daniel got to spend a little time together each evening was an extra bonus, even if they were being very efficiently chaperoned by two five-year-olds.

'I'm due out to make some house calls any minute,' he said, raising his voice over noise in the background. 'But if I take over your turn collecting the boys this afternoon and drop them off with my mother on my way, could you take over the delivery in progress over here?'

'What about the midwives? Where are they?' Sam was very careful not to tread on any departmental toes unnecessarily. Katy, Faith and Lissa were all qualified midwives as well as health visitors and, because babies rarely decided to arrive at the most convenient times, there was usually at least one on call at any time.

'One off sick, one involved in a home birth and unlikely to be finished for at least a couple of hours and the third accompanying a multiple birth who's gone into prem labour. They're at least halfway to Airedale General by now so the tinies can go straight into NICU as soon as they arrive.' The noise in the background was growing louder. It sounded almost like the high-pitched whine of a circular saw but as far as she knew there was no building going on in the Domino unit.

'So I'm the next in line, am I?' She raised her voice, too, in case he was having difficulty hearing her over the racket.

'You're certainly the most likely to be able to deal with this young lady,' he said with a touch of exasperation in his voice. 'How soon can you get here?'

Sam grimaced at the small mountain of paperwork she'd hoped to conquer before it was time to make her way to the school and shrugged her resignation. It would still be waiting here when she got back.

'Give me five minutes for a quick detour past the nearest bathroom and have a cup of coffee waiting for me when I get there,' she said and heard him chuckle as she ended the call.

She had only just stepped through the double doors leading into the Domino unit when she was stopped in her tracks by a blood-curdling scream.

Was this what she'd been able to hear in the background of Daniel's phone call?

Certain that some poor mother must be in severe difficulties, she hurried towards the delivery room, wondering why on earth Daniel hadn't warned her.

Were they going to have to rush her to the nearest general hospital if they were going to save the baby's life? Was the mother's life in jeopardy, too?

The closer she got, the easier it was to distinguish words in what had sounded a formless scream, but Sam was quite shocked when she finally stood outside the doors and caught her first glimpse of her patient.

'Get rid of it!' screamed a young girl who hardly

looked more than thirteen. 'I don't want the bloody baby! I *never* wanted a bloody baby!'

Sam was almost glad that the escalating contraction robbed the girl of the breath to continue. At least holding the Entonox mask over her face kept her occupied and helped to keep the noise down.

Sam hurried to scrub and quickly donned the green gown before shouldering her way through the doors.

She was just in time for the next foul-mouthed diatribe and couldn't help seeing the unhappy expression on the young nurse at her side.

'Shut up!' Sam commanded sharply, bringing her face just inches from the screaming girl's sweat-sheened face.

The silence was immediate, broken only by a sobbing intake of breath.

It was too good to last.

'Who the hell are you? Some bloody nurse? You can't shout at me. Just get me a doctor so I can get rid of this bloody baby.'

'I *am* a doctor,' Sam replied firmly as she glanced swiftly over the notes handed to her. 'And the only way you're going to get rid of that baby is by giving birth to it.'

'What…?'

Sam didn't allow her to get into her stride before she'd given her the options, and even with the most cursory of examinations she could see that labour was already too far advanced to make even the swiftest of epidurals ineffective.

'There are only two ways that baby is coming out—the hard way or the easy way,' she said, half-amazed to hear the words coming out of her mouth.

With that hard edge to her voice she sounded almost as bad as Dirty Harry.

She felt almost cruel to be treating such a young patient in such an apparently abrupt way, but there was no time for anything else.

It seemed to be having some sort of effect, too. At least Leanne had stopped screaming and cursing long enough to listen.

'What's the difference?' she demanded truculently, her face suddenly looking very sulky and childish in spite of the very adult situation she found herself in.

'Either you work *against* the pain or you work *with* it,' Sam said simply. 'What you've been doing is fighting the pain of your contractions. That's the hard way. You're wasting time and energy.'

She could have mentioned that she was also putting her baby at risk but, in view of her apparently violent aversion to the child she was carrying, that probably wouldn't carry much weight at the moment.

She couldn't help remembering the day Danny was born, her own mixed emotions of joy and sadness that she was finally going to be able to see Daniel's child—the only thing she had left of him except her memories. It was a strange feeling to be dealing with someone who bore her child such ill will.

'Have you been to any antenatal classes?' Sam asked, checking to find out just how much basic knowledge the girl had about what was going on inside her as she carefully examined her unnaturally slender patient.

'No fear. I didn't want all me mates to know I'd been knocked up. None of them got caught. They just think I put on weight after me and Chris split up.'

'What about your parents? Are they here?' Sam straightened up, delighted with her findings. The baby was well positioned and the head felt a good size in relation to Leanne's pelvic opening. She was also fully dilated and would probably be ready to begin pushing with the next contraction.

'God, no!' Leanne exclaimed in horror. 'They think I'm at school.'

Sam stared at her in shock.

'You mean, you came into the hospital all on your own?' The girl was a minor, for heaven's sake. As her medical attendant, did that put Sam *in loco parentis*? What on earth would that do to her malpractice insurance if something went wrong? Where was Daniel when she needed to speak to him? She had absolutely no idea which member of the hospital administrative staff she ought to speak to and there was no time to find out.

'Why shouldn't I come in by myself?' Leanne shrugged dismissively, a strangely adult gesture with such skinny childish shoulders. 'I ain't taking the kid home with me so what does it matter? This way no one will ever know it happened.'

The final words were said through gritted teeth and Sam swore silently at herself.

Instead of grilling the girl she should have been explaining what was happening and what she wanted her to do. All she could do this time was block her ears to the foul language and hope the Entonox did its job. The next contraction would be the one when Leanne really began the hard work of pushing her child out into the world. All Sam had to do was find simple enough language to convey what was needed.

'Right, Leanne, this is what is called on-the-job training,' she said briskly as soon as the contraction began to fade. She took one slender hand in hers and deliberately caught her gaze. 'All the painful waiting is over. When the next contraction comes, you'll get the feeling that you've been constipated for at least six months and you've just got to push.'

'It felt like that on the last one,' the youngster complained swiftly. 'This is just so gross.'

Sam felt it safer to ignore the comment while they seemed to be working on the same side.

'Now take a couple of good breaths to get lots of oxygen inside you. It's the oxygen in your blood that helps the muscles to work to make the pushing really strong. And the stronger the push, the fewer times you'll need to do it.'

'Thank God for that,' Leanne groaned from behind the clear plastic mask, her grimace telling Sam that the next contraction was building.

'Remember, sweetheart, no thrashing about. No screaming and cursing. Use all that energy to push the baby out.'

Leanne glared at her but she was obviously intelligent enough to see the reason behind what Sam was telling her.

In the event, it took barely fifteen minutes of concentrated effort before there was a sharp wail from the newest member of the human race.

'It's a girl,' Sam announced. 'And she's absolutely beautiful.'

Seeing the tiny wrinkled bundle in all her naked glory, the description might have seemed a little extravagant, but then Sam thought *every* new baby was beautiful.

As soon as she'd checked her over, Sam wrapped her up and stepped forward to offer her to Leanne.

In an automatic gesture as old as time the thin arms rose up to enfold her child and Leanne gazed in open fascination into her tiny face.

'She's so small,' she said in awe, not a trace of animosity in sight. 'I had a doll bigger than this when I was little.'

As Sam watched, the new baby's eyes opened, almost seeming to look straight into those of her mother.

'She's looking at me,' Leanne whispered as tears began to trickle down her face and drip onto the baby's wrap. 'Do you think she knows I'm her mother?'

Sam still got a lump in her throat when she thought about that simple question, even standing in her kitchen stirring the cheese sauce for Danny's favourite supper of macaroni cheese.

It was several hours since Leanne's parents had been called to the hospital where Sam had taken on the task of explaining the events of the day.

There had been shock and tears on all sides but when Leanne's mother had held her tiny granddaughter for the first time, Sam could tell that there was probably going to be a happy ending.

She hadn't realised just how long she had been standing there reliving recent events until she suddenly became aware of the sound of drips of water hitting the top of the kitchen cupboards and realised that Danny's bath water was still running.

CHAPTER NINE

'DANIEL JAMES TAYLOR!' Sam shouted as she took off towards the stairs at a run. 'Come here this minute!'

By the time she reached the top of the stairs she was met by a very dishevelled, sweaty little boy wearing a very puzzled look.

'Mum? What's the matter? Why did you shout at me?'

'Go down to the bottom of the stairs and wait till I tell you,' she said firmly, her ears still full of the sound of running water. 'Now, Danny. *Right now!*'

The urgency in her voice penetrated this time and he took off down the steep stairs as fast as his sturdy little legs would carry him.

Sam daren't wait to watch him. Every second she delayed meant that much more water was cascading over the side of the bath and on to the floor; that much more soaking its way through to the less than sturdy kitchen ceiling.

Sam gasped in horror when she saw the state of the bathroom. The floor looked like a shallow lake separated from her bedroom only by a single step.

There was no time for indecision. Who knew how long the ceiling could bear the weight of that many gallons of water?

She kicked off her shoes and stepped down into the water, unable to suppress a grimace when she found it was cold. Danny must have completely drained the tank of hot water.

'Such an inconvenience,' she murmured with just a touch of hysteria as she sloshed towards the gushing taps. 'It would be much nicer to wade about in warm water.'

It was strange to turn the taps off and still be left with the sound of running water, and that was *before* she pulled the plug out.

A quick glance around told her that the only container in the whole room available for baling out was the mug holding their toothbrushes.

'It may be bigger than the proverbial teaspoon, but not much better when there's this much to deal with,' she murmured in resignation and turned to wade back to her bedroom. Perhaps a saucepan and a bucket would speed things up.

She wasn't certain what happened, but one moment she was picking her way carefully through the pale blue seaweed of her bath mat and the next there was a groaning wrenching sound as almost a quarter of the floor collapsed with a jolt into the kitchen.

Sam hung on to the pedestal of the toilet, too shocked and scared to scream, almost too frightened to breathe.

In between her and the comparative safety of her bedroom was a gaping hole surrounded by the jagged edges of timber and plasterboard. She had no idea why she hadn't followed the missing part of the floor and all those gallons of water through to the lower floor. She couldn't even remember how she came to be lying full-length along one edge of the room with her arms clasped tightly around the porcelain bowl.

'The last time I got this close to a toilet was when

I had morning sickness,' she murmured as the inconsequential thought leapt into her head.

That reminded her that she still hadn't checked her diary to see how much risk she and Daniel had run with their unprotected one-night stand. Was that because she was afraid she was pregnant…or afraid that she wasn't?

'Mummy?' called a frightened little voice. 'What was that big bang?'

'Danny!' she whispered. What kind of a mother was she if she could completely forget that her child was wandering about somewhere in a partially demolished house?

'Mummy! Where are you?'

Was it her imagination or did his voice sound closer?

'Danny, don't come upstairs!' she ordered firmly. 'You *must* stay in the sitting room. I want you to go to the telephone and dial nine-nine-nine, just like we practised. Can you do that for me?'

'Yes. I can!' he said eagerly, then the significance of the request seemed to register with him. 'Is there a fire, Mum?' he demanded, clearly concerned.

'Not with all this water around,' she muttered under her breath then continued aloud. 'No, sweetheart. No fire, but we're going to need the fireman to bring his engine to get all this water out.' She wasn't going to frighten him with the details of her own plight.

There were all sorts of ominous creaks and cracks going on around her while she tried to hear what Danny was saying. Was it just the sound of everything settling down after the cataclysm, or was her narrow perch going to disappear at any moment?

It seemed like a very long time before she heard his precious voice again.

'Mum? Can you hear me?'

'I can hear you, Danny.' She could hear him all too well with the hole beside her leading straight into the kitchen. 'Stay in the sitting room, sweetheart. Did you make the call?'

'I did it!' he exclaimed, full of importance. 'But they asked me where we live and I could only remember our old road.'

Sam groaned silently and rested her forehead on one trembling arm. How could she have been so stupid! She'd completely forgotten to teach him their new address.

'What did they say?'

She forced herself to keep her voice cheerful when all she wanted to do was cry. Heaven knew what Danny would do if he heard his mother crying—probably come up to see what was the matter. Then there would be two of them in danger.

'They asked if we had a neighbour or a friend and I said we had Jamie's dad.'

'And did you tell them who Jamie's dad is?' She could just imagine the emergency services trying to track down someone called Jamie's dad.

'Of course I did.' He sounded quite indignant and she could imagine the expression on his little face all too easily. 'I said he's a doctor at the hospital and his name is the same as mine. Daniel James.'

Because you were named after him, sweetheart, she longed to say, and regret clutched at her heart.

She suddenly realised, when she was staring into the uncertainty of the next few minutes, that it was time that she and Daniel made some far-reaching decisions. The most important was that Danny had the right to know who his real father was.

It had been weeks, now, since she'd discovered that Daniel hadn't died five years ago. Why on earth had she been hesitating all this time?

So what if Daniel hadn't been able to be faithful to one woman at a time? He had certainly proved that he was willing to take care of his child. She only had to look at Jamie to see what a good job he was making of fatherhood.

What if she hadn't been lucky enough to grab hold of her ignominious handhold when the floor gave way? What if, at this very moment, she was lying dead on the kitchen floor? What would it be like for Danny to find out after her death that she'd kept such an important fact from him?

She didn't have any doubt that Daniel would take care of him, the way he had Jamie.

It was all so blindingly simple, really, and right then she made herself a promise that if…*when* she was safe again, she was going to tell Daniel that she wanted Danny to know the truth about his parentage.

In the most fundamental way, it didn't matter whether she and Daniel ever managed to achieve any degree of permanence. It didn't matter if her heart broke because she couldn't have the man she loved. What mattered was Danny's happiness and security.

Suddenly, it was as if a great burden had lifted and she felt almost light-hearted.

Buoyed by her decision, Sam closed her eyes and concentrated on staying calm.

Danny had delegated himself to watch at the sitting room window for the fire engine to arrive. All she could do now was hope that he had given the emergency services enough information so that they could find the cottage. If someone was able to fathom who 'Jamie's dad' was, Daniel would be able to give them the right address.

Sam was shivering uncontrollably by the time she heard the sound of adult voices, a reaction to the combination of shock at her narrow escape and being soaked to the skin.

It hadn't helped that she'd been lying in the same position for such a long time with her arms wrapped around a cold toilet bowl, either. She certainly hadn't dared to move enough to keep her circulation going.

'Sam? Can you hear me?' called a voice and she was sure she must have started to hallucinate.

'Daniel?' she whispered. Was this a case of wishful thinking?

'Sam?' She heard his voice getting closer and realised he was making his way towards the kitchen.

'Daniel,' she croaked and desperately tried to clear her throat. 'Daniel! Don't open the door!'

'What? Where are you?' he demanded but she was glad to hear that he wasn't coming any closer. 'Sam, the hallway's full of water. What's happened? Danny rang for the fire brigade and they contacted me.'

'I'm upstairs, but part of the bathroom ceiling fell down into the kitchen when the bath overflowed. Don't go into the kitchen. Something might fall on you.'

'Upstairs? Sam, where are you exactly?' There was a scuffling sound and from her position on one side of the bathroom floor she could just see the shape of his head as he peered around the edge of the kitchen door.

She'd never been so glad to see anyone in her whole life.

'Hello, Daniel,' she said in a voice made shakier still by her overflowing emotions. 'I'm up here.'

Sam never bothered to find out exactly how the fire crew managed to get her out of the ruined bathroom without a hitch. All she was interested in was listening to Daniel's voice as he kept up a steady stream of conversation while everything went on around them.

When she was carried out on a stretcher, strapped to a backboard, her neck in a collar, wrapped up like an Egyptian mummy and protesting all the way, Daniel was waiting for her with Danny in his arms.

'There you are, Dan my man. Mummy's safe and they're just going to take her to the hospital to make sure she hasn't hurt anything.'

'I'm sorry, Mummy…about forgetting the taps.' From his penitent expression he'd obviously worked out what had caused the disaster.

'You made up for it by making that important phone call, and watching out for the fire engine to come,' she pointed out softly, accentuating the positive aspects of his involvement.

She was just so overwhelmingly grateful that he hadn't been injured. If he'd been in the kitchen when the ceiling fell through…

She shuddered.

'Mum? Where are you going to sleep? At the hospital?' he demanded, his deep blue eyes bright with curiosity. 'Jamie's dad says I can stay in Jamie's bunk bed, but there isn't room for you.'

'If he can start with a list of questions like that,

he obviously won't be suffering any permanent emotional damage over the incident,' Daniel said dryly as he put Danny down again. 'Don't worry, I'll take him home safely.'

'I know you will. You love him, don't you.' It wasn't a question.

'Yes, I do,' he confirmed quietly and she gave a shaky smile.

She was loaded into the waiting ambulance more convinced than ever that she'd made the right decision.

An hour later she was convinced that the staff in the accident and emergency unit were deliberately tormenting her because she was a member of staff. It didn't matter that Jack Lawrence was single and the second-best-looking doctor on the staff nor that he was a consummate flirt.

She'd been poked and prodded and examined from every conceivable angle and was embarrassed to know that she'd raised more than one set of eyebrows when she'd firmly refused to have any x-rays taken.

'It's not necessary, Trish,' she declared, her level of frustration rising with every second. 'I was just cold and wet and my arms are going to be stiff as wooden boards in the morning from hugging the damn toilet for an hour or so. I haven't fallen and nothing has fallen on me. I will *not* be x-rayed unnecessarily.'

The fact that she still hadn't checked her dates after her night with Daniel had absolutely nothing to do with it, she told herself self-righteously. *Any* conscientious doctor would avoid unnecessary irradiation.

'Do I take it you don't want to stay here any more?' asked a familiar voice and she could have wept with relief.

'No. I don't,' she snapped crossly. 'I don't ever want to come near this place again. They all take an evil delight in putting innocent people through sadistic and unnecessary routines.'

At least her tirade had made everybody laugh, but it was the gentle expression in Daniel's eyes that captured her.

'Let's go home, then,' he said and bent to swing her up in his arms.

'Daniel!' she squeaked, her cheeks growing hot as she heard the sound of laughter following them out of the door. 'I *can* walk, you know.'

'And I can carry you,' he retorted calmly and continued across to his car. 'Humour me.'

'Humour you?' she repeated when he slid behind the wheel having deposited her into her seat as carefully as if she were a Dresden china figurine.

'Yes. Humour me.' His voice was rough as he turned towards her in the distorted light thrown out by the street lights around the car park. 'When I saw you on that jagged patch of bathroom floor, hanging on to the toilet, for heaven's sake…!'

He drew in a steadying breath as he reached out to touch her cheek and she could see the way his hand trembled.

'I suddenly realised exactly how close you came to dying or, at least, being seriously injured—so, yes, humour me because I'm just grateful that you're alive.'

He turned away then and concentrated on starting

the engine as though uncomfortable with his loss of control.

Sam wondered whether he realised just how much of his emotions he'd revealed and it was several minutes before she realised which road he was taking.

'You're going the wrong way,' she pointed out softly. 'The cottage is…'

'I know where the cottage is,' he muttered savagely. 'But if you think I'd take you somewhere that dangerous, you've got another think coming. I'm taking you home with me.'

Sam's hackles rose at his tone.

She'd decided when her marriage to Andrew had foundered that she wasn't going to allow other people to make her decisions for her any more.

Perhaps she could blame it on the traumas of the day but she should have known when it was safer to stay silent.

'And did you ask me if I wanted to come to your home?' she challenged. 'Did you ask your mother if it was convenient?'

He was silent for a beat.

'Sam,' he said softly. 'Don't. Not tonight.'

There was something in his tone that made her subside and she held her tongue until he switched the engine off in front of his house.

'You did warn your mother?' she ventured, increasingly uncomfortable with the idea of being an unwanted guest.

'What do you think?' he asked with a gesture towards the front door.

In the time that she'd looked away the door had been flung open so that a wide swathe of light spilled out onto the gravel driveway. Standing on the top step waiting to welcome her stood Joyce Hennessy.

'Oh, my dear. Such a thing to happen,' she exclaimed as soon as Sam was close enough. 'Are you sure you're really all right? Did the hospital check you over properly? Do you want Daniel to…?'

'Mother!' her son chided. 'You're going to have to give up fussing over her. You haven't seen this woman when she gets her temper up. You should have seen what she did to the poor staff at the hospital when they dared to suggest taking some x-rays. You'd have thought they were suggesting major surgery!'

'I'm sure she did no such thing,' she retorted and led the way into the cosy house. 'Still, it must have been a terrible ordeal, my dear. Daniel will show you the way and I'll bring you some supper on a tray in a few minutes. You could look in on the boys on the way, if you want to.'

Daniel shrugged wryly as his mother bustled off towards the kitchen.

'Obviously my bossiness was genetically inherited,' he said smugly and gestured for her to start up the stairs.

If it weren't for the fact that she couldn't wait to see her son, she might have argued with him, but as it was she meekly complied.

It was the first time she had seen the famous bunk beds that Danny coveted so highly. In the wash of light from the hallway she could see that the whole room definitely belonged to a boy, with brightly coloured posters decorating the walls and action toys on every available surface. Even the beds were decorated with duvet covers printed with cartoon characters.

She stepped forward silently, peering through the subdued light at each face in turn.

She still wasn't accustomed to how much alike they looked, even after seeing them together on an almost daily basis. The same dark hair with a tendency to curl when it grew too long, the same hint of a dimple in one cheek, the same boyish chubbiness covering a strong bone structure that would mature into their father's good looks.

'Sometimes I can't get over how alike they look,' Daniel whispered. 'It's a good job their teacher can tell them apart or they'd probably be getting up to all sorts of tricks.'

The reason why the two of them looked so alike was something that she and Daniel still had to discuss, and the reminder suddenly sapped her of what little energy she had left.

She bent forward to the lower bunk and pressed a soft kiss to Danny's forehead. With a whispered, 'Good night', she straightened then found herself reaching out to smooth a gentle hand over Jamie's tousled hair. It wasn't his fault that his father had been a little profligate with his favours and Sam had never believed in the sins of the father being visited on the sons.

She followed Daniel out of the room and through the next door along the corridor.

Once inside, she froze in surprise.

'But this is *your* room!' she exclaimed. Her surprise was tempered by intrigue. If she'd been interested in Jamie's room, she was fascinated by

Daniel's. This was where he spent nearly one third of his life.

'Don't blame me for the choice of rooms. This was my mother's suggestion,' he revealed with an attempt at defensiveness.

Now she was really shocked.

'Your mother expects us to sleep together?' Her eyes went wide as they flew from his to the mesmerising width of the enormous double bed that dominated the room.

She could imagine all too easily how he would look sprawled across it, even though it was more than five years since she'd last witnessed the sight. It was an image indelibly printed in her mind among her treasured memories.

'No. Unfortunately, she doesn't expect us to share it,' he corrected her huskily, and the expression in his deep blue eyes spoke volumes.

Sam was glad she didn't have to admit to her disappointment out loud, but she was suddenly sure that he knew. If her cheeks had been pale before, the heat she could feel in them now was silent proof of the direction of her thoughts.

Daniel shifted his weight from one foot to the other and cleared his throat.

'The bathroom is through there.' He gestured towards the doorway on the other side of the room. 'It's actually a shower, but you won't have to share it with the children. I know they dried you off at the hospital but you'll probably want to get rid of the plaster dust before you get into bed. Let me know if you need any help scrubbing your back...!'

With a wink and a brief sexy grin he left the room.

Sam blew out a silent whistle and tentatively

perched on the nearest corner of the bed. What that man did to her blood pressure and pulse rate, to say nothing of her knees...

Without him there to watch her every move, she took her time looking around.

In its own way the room and its furniture were unremarkable. Plain solid wood the colour of dark honey gleamed softly where the light caught it, and the overall colour scheme of ivory and French navy was warmed by touches of rich burgundy red.

It was obviously a man's room, right down to the leather belt draped over the denim jeans folded on the back of a chair and the scruffy trainers abandoned in front of the wardrobe.

She was unaccountably relieved to see that there wasn't a single piece of evidence that he'd ever shared the room with another woman—not that he was exactly sharing it with her...

There was a framed photo of Joyce Hennessy holding a little baby who could only be Jamie but, as to Jamie's mother, there wasn't a trace.

The sound of Daniel's voice somewhere in the distance snapped her out of her inspection and sent her hurrying towards the bathroom. Joyce had said she would have some food ready in a few minutes and heaven only knew how long she'd been sitting there in baggy theatre greens gawping.

She chuckled aloud as she shed her borrowed clothes in a heap.

Gawping?

She hadn't used that word for years, not even in her thoughts. It was a real throwback to her childhood days in Edenthwaite.

Her arms already felt stiff and achy but she'd

shampooed and scrubbed until she felt blissfully clean and warm before she realised that she didn't have anything other than the discarded theatre greens to put on. Until she climbed out of the shower and found a thick navy towelling robe and an oversized white T-shirt draped over the towel rail.

She knew they hadn't been there when she came into the bathroom and every inch of her tingled at the realisation that Daniel had come into the room while she was naked under the shower.

It wasn't the first time they'd been in a bathroom together and certainly wasn't the first time he would have seen her naked but, for some reason, there was a different intimacy to it this time.

'Supper is served,' Daniel intoned in his best impression of an upper-class butler and Sam squeaked as she hurriedly reached for the T-shirt.

It was one thing to stand there in the privacy of the bathroom mooning about his thoughtfulness at providing her with temporary clothing while wondering if he'd peeped at her naked body through the frosted glass panels of the shower. It was another thing entirely to have him walk in on her when she was standing there stark naked with a besotted expression on her face.

'Mum made you an omelette,' Daniel announced with a gesture towards the well-laden tray when she padded barefooted into his bedroom.

Her heart did a silly little jig when she saw he was still there, apparently waiting for her.

He'd placed the tray on the bedside cabinet and was now sprawled in the chair with his head tipped back against the jeans draped over the back of it.

He straightened effortlessly out of the chair and

came towards her. 'Will you be more comfortable sitting on the side of the bed or do you want to get under the covers?'

She was still thinking about those words when she pulled the covers up to her chin and tried to compose herself to sleep.

Yes, she'd wanted to get under the covers, but not just to eat her supper, delicious as it was. What she wanted to do was grab the man and pull him under the covers with her.

Was it a natural human reaction to her close brush with death or was it just her hormones going into overdrive because they recognised their mate?

Whatever it was, the bed felt far too big and lonely, especially when she could smell the scent of Daniel's soap and shampoo all around her mixed with the indefinable musk that belonged to him alone.

She'd expected to find it hard to sleep, expecting her subconscious to erect all sorts of nightmare memories as soon as she closed her eyes, but it didn't happen.

Whether she was just too exhausted, or whether it was the sense of security she felt lying in Daniel's bed she found herself drifting inexorably into slumber.

The room was still dark when she woke, certain she'd heard a sound.

Was that Danny? Was he ill?

She reached out to switch on the bedside light but it wasn't there.

She was still frowning when she suddenly remembered what had happened this evening—or was it yesterday?—and realised where she was.

She heard another sound, just a soft one, over in the corner of the room and peered into the shadows.

That was where Daniel's chair was. She could just see the outline of it, with the jeans folded over the back.

The noise came again and she fumbled around until she finally found the bedside light where it had been pushed back to accommodate her supper tray.

And then she saw Daniel and her heart melted. He was slumped down in the chair and fast asleep, the uncomfortable angle of his head making him snore softly.

It might have been the click of the switch or even the soft wash of light reaching him, but as she watched he opened sleepy eyes.

'Are you all right?' His low murmur sounded almost rusty and utterly sexy. She watched him grimace when he tried to move and found the crick in his neck.

Before she could censor the words on the tip of her tongue she had said them.

'If you come over here I could rub that better for you.' She hadn't intended to sound so seductive but the sharp expression in his eyes told her that was the way he had taken her offer.

For just a moment she thought he was going to accept the invitation, the dark heat of his eyes sending her pulse into overdrive, then he shook his head.

'I think it's safer if I stay over here,' he murmured wryly. 'There are rather too many chaperones in the house to take any risks, and if I joined you on that bed...'

He didn't need to say any more. Her imagination and her memories could supply the rest. Unfortunately, her imagination and her memories were still working overtime when the light was switched off again and the knowledge that Daniel was only on the other side of the room made it very much harder to fall asleep again.

CHAPTER TEN

'HE SHOULD have woken me when Danny got up,' Sam said politely but firmly when Joyce woke her up the next morning with a cup of tea.

'Danny needed clean clothes for school and I've got a surgery to take,' she continued, then exasperation took over. 'The wretched man *knows* I don't like people taking over and organising my life. I've had enough of that in the past.'

She shut her mouth with a snap to stop any more words escaping then bit her lip and wondered how badly Daniel's mother would take the criticism of a son she clearly adored.

'Jamie's got plenty of spare clothes,' Joyce said dismissively, apparently totally unaffected by Sam's outburst. 'Daniel decided he had time to drop them both off at school on his way into the practice. He's letting them know he's going to take over your list for today and those two lads were perfectly happy setting their day off together. They actually said they'd like to do it more often,' she added, and the glance she threw Sam was full of speculation.

Sam wasn't touching that topic with a barge pole until she'd spoken to Daniel.

That was the discussion she'd hoped to have this morning, if only he'd woken her up in time. She'd lain awake for several hours after he'd begun that gentle snoring again, working out exactly what she wanted to say.

Now she only had twenty minutes to get herself washed and dressed to be ready at her desk on time for her first patient.

Impossible. Especially without a stitch of clean clothing to her name and her car parked in front of the cottage.

'I'm sorry if I sound ungrateful, but…could I use your phone? I'm going to need to phone the GP unit to warn them I'm going to be late, and then I want to arrange for a taxi so I can get to my car.'

Joyce regarded her silently for a moment then smiled broadly.

'You'll do nicely!' she exclaimed cryptically then pointed at the cup of tea. 'Get that inside you while you make your call to the surgery then fling those green pyjama things on. I'll be making you a slice of toast to eat in the car. It'll be much quicker if *I'm* your taxi driver.'

She bustled off towards the door and suddenly whirled back to face Sam, chuckling aloud.

'That lad of mine sometimes gets his own way far too easily. It'll do him good to have someone stand up to him.'

It was a nice feeling, knowing that Daniel's mother was an ally. She obviously had her own agenda where the well-being of her newly-discovered grandson was concerned, and Sam was more than inclined to go along with her. What she didn't know was whether Daniel's agenda matched.

'Good morning!' Paula Smith, formerly Skillington, greeted Sam as she strode through the main doors. 'I arrive back from my honeymoon to find there's been high excitement going on while I was away. Fire brigade. Ambulance. Flood. Daring rescue of damsel in distress. Have you got time to tell me all about it?'

'Sorry, not this morning, Paula. I'm already late for the start of surgery,' Sam said with a preoccupied smile as she made for the East wing housing the GP unit with firm steps.

Today was the beginning of the rest of her life, and she was starting as she meant to go on, she repeated silently as she made her way towards the practice reception desk.

There had been a letter waiting for her when Joyce had delivered her to her less than pristine home a little while ago. She'd recognised Andrew's atrocious writing on the envelope, and the post office addition showing that it had been forwarded from her previous address.

She had no idea why he needed to write to her. They hadn't been in contact since the divorce was finalised. She hadn't actually intended opening it until later in the day, when she might have more time, but something had prompted her and she'd ended up slitting it open just before she left the house.

It was a single sheet of paper covered with his dreadfully illegible doctor's scrawl announcing that he had remarried a fortnight ago, that his new wife was expecting his child in about seven months and that he hoped Sam wished him well.

A month ago, that letter would have sent her into a depression as she remembered the hell they'd put each other through during their misguided marriage.

Since she'd found out that Daniel was still alive her whole attitude had changed and she was glad of this evidence that he'd been able to put it all behind him, too. Today she found she really could wish him well in his new life and the realisation had put an extra spring in her step.

'Good morning,' Anne Townsend said with a discreet nod when Sam finally made it to the GP unit reception area. 'I'll send your next patient through in a couple of minutes, shall I?'

'That'll do nicely, thank you,' Sam said with a sincere smile, grateful that the senior receptionist was experienced enough to read between the lines without having to comment. She'd clearly been surprised when Sam had phoned to warn her that she *was* going to be coming in to work but would be a little late. She had obviously made an intelligent guess at what exactly was going on when Sam had countermanded Daniel's arrangements.

Now all she had to do was wait for the man himself to realise that she was perfectly well able to decide if she was fit to go to work. It shouldn't take long if her patients were being diverted back to her.

She had Jason Caddick in with her when she heard Daniel's raised voice through the wall separating their rooms and couldn't help the little smile that lifted the corners of her mouth. He didn't sound particularly happy with the news he'd just received and his reaction reminded her all too clearly of a certain miniature version of the man.

Jason was another matter entirely. His personality almost seemed to have grown since his illness had been diagnosed. It was hard to realise that he was still barely eighteen years old; he seemed so much more mature somehow than the frightened young lad who'd come to see her just a few weeks ago.

Apparently, it hadn't been long after he started

chemotherapy that his hair started falling out in handfuls.

'I'd lost so much that I opted to shave the rest off. Well, it was that or look like I'd been attacked by moths. Dad suggested I wear a hat, but I'm going bareheaded on purpose,' he said with a grin. 'I told him it was so he could get used to the sight for what he'll see in the mirror when he goes completely bald!'

'You rotten toad! He's only going a bit thin at the front!' she exclaimed, unable to suppress a chuckle of her own.

Secretly, she was amazed by his indomitable spirit. If there were any guarantees of success against this disease based on the patient's will to overcome it, Jason was a prime candidate. It was almost as if he'd taken the leukaemia on as a personal intellectual challenge.

'When I've beaten this thing,' he said, his tone as positive as his words, 'I've decided that I'm going to specialise in this field. Do you realise that before treatment was available, most people who had ALL were dead within four months of diagnosis? Now, they can actually talk about a cure rate. Ninety per cent go into first remission, and there's a better than fifty per cent chance of having no sign of the disease five years later.'

Sam surreptitiously crossed her fingers and sent a silent prayer winging up that he would be one of the lucky ones.

Unfortunately, only time would tell, and if her conversation with Daniel didn't go the way she wanted, she might not be here to find out what happened to Jason.

It was another two hours before she bade farewell to the last person on her list.

She'd heard Daniel's voice at intervals during the morning and knew he was still on the premises so she was half expecting the next knock on her door. It still made her jump.

'Feeling happier now you've put in a full morning?' Daniel asked blandly as he deposited the two steaming mugs he'd carried in one hand on to her desk then picked one up again and blew on the surface as he sat down.

'Much happier,' she said with a deliberately sweet smile and a nod of thanks for the coffee. 'I do like being busy. Did you know that Leanne's decided to keep the baby? Her mother's going to help her look after it while she finishes school.'

'I heard,' he said shortly, obviously slightly uneasy with the way this meeting was going.

What had he expected? A screaming match? That wasn't her style.

'I also saw Mark and Janet Ashland first thing this morning,' he volunteered. 'They came in expecting to show you the baby and ended up telling me all about your box of mirrors.'

'Is it still working?' Sam demanded, totally forgetting to keep up the calm front in her eagerness to find out how the poor tormented man was faring.

Daniel's 'gotcha' grin before he gave her the glowing report was enough to start the barriers crumbling. How could she not respond when she loved him so much?

'I'm sorry,' he said suddenly, completely taking the wind out of her sails. 'I should have asked you whether you felt up to coming in today, not presumed. I know you don't like people organising your life.'

The words were such an accurate echo of what she'd said to Joyce this morning that she couldn't help chuckling.

'I gather your mother put a flea in your ear,' she said wryly, knowing the older woman was as bad as her son at trying to arrange things to her own liking. She'd obviously decided that matters between her son and the mother of his child needed a nudge.

'A whole family of fleas is more like it,' he admitted wryly. 'She said it was time I remembered that I can't treat everyone as if they were a patient, handing them out advice and edicts and expecting blind obedience.'

'Sounds like good advice.' Sam sipped her coffee and wondered how they were going to get from here to the topic she really wanted to broach. She could hardly bring Daniel's parentage up out of the blue.

'Sam, I think it would be a good idea if Danny was told that I'm his father,' Daniel announced suddenly, almost as if he'd been reading her mind.

She gazed at him in mute surprise.

'I promise I won't say anything to him if you're against it, but it would make a lot of sense to get the legalities sorted out,' he continued in his most persuasive tones. 'I've been thinking about it ever since I found out about him but it was the accident last night that convinced me.'

He was on a roll, now, and as he was only saying the things she'd been thinking, too, she let him continue.

'If anything serious were to happen to you, it would mean that the courts couldn't prevent me taking care of him. It would also make things easier for my mother. She already loves him to pieces and she's dying to tell him she's his grandmother.

'He's bound to find out, anyway, if you're going to be staying in the area,' he pointed out anxiously when she still didn't interrupt. 'People aren't daft and with him and Jamie looking like two peas from the same pod one day someone's going to make a comment that he hears. It *must* be better if we explain everything rather than have him find out by accident. He might think I haven't said anything because I didn't want him and...'

'I agree,' she said quietly, finally cutting him off in mid-flow as effectively as if she'd shouted.

'You agree?' He leant back in the chair with a thump. 'Just like that? No argument?'

'Just like that. No argument,' she repeated serenely. 'Actually, that's one of the reasons why I was so stewed that you hadn't woken me up this morning for work. I'd come to the same decision and I was going to suggest it while there wasn't anyone else around to overhear the discussion.'

'Thank God for that.' He closed his eyes and heaved a sigh of relief.

'You weren't expecting it to be that easy?' she teased gently.

'Nothing with you is ever easy,' he retorted darkly, his brows drawn down ferociously over deep blue eyes that gleamed with a seductive mixture of relief and pleasure.

'Nothing worthwhile ever is,' she added seriously, remembering her deliberations last night.

Her heart was already committed to Daniel, but before she could be certain that she had a place in his everyday life, she'd wanted to ask him about Jamie's mother and her present position in their lives.

This morning she'd realised that she already knew the most important answer.

A man as honourable as Daniel—one who would condemn himself to an uncomfortable night in a chair to watch over her when there had been an open invitation to join her in the bed—couldn't possibly have done something as crass as made her pregnant while he was already involved with Jamie's mother.

There must be another answer.

'Daniel, what happened to Jamie's mother?' she asked, realising that it was time she finally screwed her courage up. 'I've never heard you mention her, not even her name.'

He frowned. The question was obviously coming at him from an unexpected direction and he didn't seem to be able to see the connection with their conversation.

'Didn't my mother tell you what happened?' He sounded quite surprised. 'I thought the two of you would have taken the chance this morning to have a good long gossip.'

'I've never been much of a one for gossip,' she said wryly. 'In fact, my biggest mistakes have probably been as a result of trying to avoid it.'

He was quick on the uptake.

'Your marriage?'

She nodded. 'My parents went ballistic when I told them about Danny. You can imagine what the news that their daughter was unmarried and pregnant would do to them in a place like Edenthwaite.'

'So you got married as soon as you could to stop the tongues wagging.' It was his turn to nod and his eyes were full of understanding. 'So, how did your mother take your divorce?'

'Don't ask. We're barely on speaking terms, yet, and one of the main reasons I came home was to be close enough to help her when she has her hip replacement. She's due to go into hospital in a couple of weeks so I'm not holding out too much hope that the waters will have magically calmed by then.'

To her frustration she realised that they'd drifted a long way from what she wanted to know *and* she'd run out of coffee. Still, she wasn't going to go to the staff room for another cup until she had her answer.

'One day she'll be glad that you kept trying to mend the bridges,' he promised with a special conviction in his tone. 'That call from my brother was the one that mended them between the two of us, so I couldn't refuse him when he needed help, even though it couldn't have been at a worse time for me.'

Sam remembered all too clearly that Daniel had been just weeks away from some major exams, and then there was their relationship as well.

'We'd argued about him signing up to go back for another stint abroad when Maggie was pregnant…'

'Maggie?' she interrupted. She was sure she hadn't heard that name before, but…

James' wife? Jamie's mother! All of a sudden, before Daniel could get the words out, it all fitted together.

'His wife.' Daniel smiled sadly, reminiscently, as he unwittingly confirmed what she had finally worked out for herself. 'She wasn't even as tall as you—probably barely five feet—but she was a real bulldog about getting her own way.'

Sam's glare dared him to make the comparison.

'I told James that he was mad to let her go with him when things were looking so dicey and he told me to keep my nose out of it.'

He broke off, clearly reliving the events, and in spite of the fact that she knew tragedy was to follow, Sam found herself waiting almost with bated breath for him to continue.

'He phoned from some godforsaken hole in the middle of nowhere and told me I'd been right. He asked me to come and get Maggie out to safety before the baby arrived.'

'But?' she prompted. She already knew what had happened to his brother but she'd never known about Maggie.

'But,' he repeated heavily. 'But I arrived just one day too late and the rebels had already struck. James was dead and Maggie was barely alive. She'd been attacked when she'd tried to defend James and then she'd gone into premature labour.' His voice cracked.

'Oh, Daniel,' she breathed. There was no way she could stay on the other side of her desk when he was that upset. She had to go to him; to make contact in the hope that it would somehow make the pain more bearable.

She took his hand but when she would have crouched beside him he pulled her onto his knee and wrapped both arms around her before he continued.

'Jamie was small but he was a fighter and I was pretty certain he would survive, but Maggie...' He shook his head. 'I would have sworn that she would have fought, too, but without James she said it just didn't seem worth it and she gave up trying.'

'So you had to deal with both their deaths while

all that mayhem was going on all around you?' She suppressed a shudder when she realised exactly how much danger he could have been in. The television reports at the time had been far too sketchy to give the true picture.

'Luckily for Jamie and I, once the rebels had got their hands on all the supplies there was no reason for them to hang around. They were in a hurry to convert their loot into the next consignment of guns and ammunition so they just torched the place and left.'

He was silent for a long moment, his cheek pressed to the top of her head, before he continued.

'I didn't think things could get any worse and then I came home to find you'd just got married.'

The desolation in his voice nearly had her in tears. If she'd ever doubted that he'd loved her more than five long years ago, she had her answer now.

'I'm so sorry,' she whispered. 'Sorry for so many things. If only I'd tried to contact you sooner. If only I'd scraped myself together to go to the funeral. If only I'd waited a bit longer before I grasped at the straw Andrew held out.'

'If only you'd divorced as soon as you realised you'd made a mistake. If only you'd kept in touch with my mother. If only you'd come home sooner...' He drew in a much-needed breath before he continued. 'Then there are all my regrets. If only I'd got my mother to keep in contact with you while I was away. If only I'd taken care of that funeral letter myself. If only I'd confronted you when I found out you'd just married... We could go on forever but it wouldn't make a bit of difference to who we are and where we are today.'

Sam nodded then settled her head back in its comfortable niche on his shoulder.

'So. What next…?'

'So. Where do we go from here…?'

They both began together and broke off with a laugh.

'Who goes first?' Daniel asked. 'Ladies before gentlemen?'

'How about age before beauty?' she countered swiftly, her heart immeasurably lighter now they were really talking again.

'I don't mind who begins as long as we come to the same conclusions,' he said quietly. 'Before James phoned me I'd made up my mind to ask you out for a special meal. I'd known that I was in love with you. I fully intended proposing to you and I wasn't going to take no for an answer.'

'Oh, Daniel. I wouldn't have said no. I loved you far too much.'

'*Loved*,' he repeated pointedly, his deep blue eyes catching and holding her gaze as though he wanted to see right inside her head. 'That's the past tense. What would your answer be now?'

'That depends on the question,' she prompted with a quiver to her voice. 'You've only told me about what you were intending to do *then*. You've never actually asked me.'

'I've already said that nothing with you is ever easy,' he grumbled as he heaved himself up out of the chair with her still in his arms then deposited her on the seat instead. 'You're really going to insist that I do this properly, aren't you?'

'Yes, please,' she said smiling through the sudden

tears of happiness that began to fill her eyes when he went down on one knee in front of her.

'I shall use the words I was going to say all those years ago. Samantha Mary Denison, I'll love you forever. Will you do me the honour of accepting my proposal of marriage?'

'Oh, yes, Daniel.' She threw her arms around him not knowing whether to laugh or cry. 'Yes, please.'

The two of them were so busy sealing her acceptance with a kiss that they were totally oblivious to the knock on the door. As it was, they only realised that they had an audience when Frankie declared, 'And about time, too. Hey, everybody, look what I've found!'

'Whose decision was this?' Daniel grumbled as he and his mother tried to keep two very lively little five-year-olds under control in the Registry office antechamber.

'Yours, dear, once Sam had told you what you'd decided,' Joyce said with a smug grin as he groaned again.

'I suppose I'm going to have to get used to living with two manipulative women, now,' he complained, but he couldn't hide his smile completely, not from the only woman who had known him all his life.

Nothing worthwhile is ever easy, Sam had said just two weeks ago on the day he'd finally proposed, and here they were after a fortnight of manic activity waiting for her to arrive.

Of course, she'd pointed out that they'd had other choices rather than doing everything in such a rush.

'We could wait until my mother's recovered from the replacement surgery on her hip,' she'd begun, the soul of sweet reason. 'That will be about three months, to make sure she'll be all right. But, by then this will have expanded into an easily recognisable bump, and I don't think she'd ever get over the public humiliation of her daughter being visibly pregnant at *both* of her weddings.'

She smiled up at him as he leant back against the headboard of her narrow single bed and continued, 'That would mean postponing the wedding until *after* the baby's arrived and hiding it whenever the photographer's around so it doesn't give the game away.'

'All right! I give in!' He threw both hands up in the air. 'There is no way that I'm waiting another six months. Another two weeks of making love in this wretched little bed is going to give me a permanent crick in my neck as it is.'

She opened her mouth to speak but he hastily put his hand over it.

'I know! It's my scruples that won't let me "cohabit" in a decent-sized bed when there are two impressionable boys around.'

'But I love your scruples!' she declared with a teasing pout as she walked her fingers across his chest through the silky thicket of dark hair. 'They're part of you.'

'I'd far rather you were part of me,' he said softly, fervently as he captured her hand and placed it over her newly discovered pregnancy. 'And the sooner the better for everyone concerned.'

Sam had finally remembered to check her diary and a swiftly administered test had confirmed the existence of the brand new life that just seemed to make the situation better. The fact that the senior partners in the GP unit at Denison Memorial had offered her a permanent post in the practice had merely put the icing on the cake.

'I wonder if it'll be a girl this time,' she mused idly, held securely against the steady beat of his heart. 'I quite like the idea of the next one being a change of sex. Your mother and I need some reinforcements to make the numbers even. And don't even think about christening her Danielle. Three of you called Daniel James are quite enough. Thank God you all answer to different variations.'

He chuckled, but he could already envisage problems sorting out which letters had been sent to who, especially when Danny's name was finally changed to Hennessy.

His smile was teasing as he looked down at her. 'You mean, you'd like the chance to come home and trip over Barbie dolls instead of Action Man?'

She gazed up at him and realised anew just how lucky she'd been. If she hadn't applied for the post at Denison Memorial she would never have known that Daniel was still alive and this child just developing deep inside her would never have been created.

'To be perfectly honest, Daniel, the sex of the baby and even how many we have isn't as important as having you in my life,' she said softly, her whole heart in her words as she gazed up at his deep blue eyes. 'What I'm most looking forward to is the chance of coming home to you every night.'

'Coming home,' he echoed as he brushed his lips over hers, and that was just what it felt like.

MILLS & BOON®

Makes any time special™

Mills & Boon publish 29 new titles every month. Select from...

Modern Romance™   Tender Romance™

Sensual Romance™

Medical Romance™   Historical Romance™

MAT2

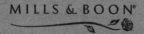

Medical Romance™

REDEEMING DR HAMMOND *by Meredith Webber*

Busy obstetrician Mitch Hammond was in desperate
need of some order in his life. Beautiful and determined
Riley Dennison agreed—Mitch needed redeeming—but
now she had to convince him that she would be perfect
as his bride!

AN ANGEL IN HIS ARMS *by Jennifer Taylor*

After the trauma in Dr Matthew Dempster's past he'd
shut everything else out, not wanting to love and lose
again. But could paramedic Sharon Lennard persuade
Matthew to let her into his life and together find the
love they both richly deserved?

THE PARAMEDIC'S SECRET *by Lilian Darcy*

When a powerful attraction flows between Anna
Brewster and her new air ambulance colleague Finn
McConnell, she knows she's in for trouble—especially
as it seems Anna's cousin is expecting his baby.
Somehow she has to resist...

On sale 6th July 2001

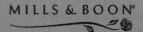

MILLS & BOON®

Medical Romance™

THE CONSULTANT'S CONFLICT *by Lucy Clark*

Book one of the McElroys trilogy

Orthopaedic surgeon Jed McElroy refused to see past Dr Sally Bransford's privileged background and acknowledge her merits. He fought his attraction to her, but as they worked side by side, the prospect of making her a McElroy was becoming irresistible!

THE PREGNANT DOCTOR *by Margaret Barker*

Highdale Practice

Dr Adam Young had supported GP Patricia Drayton at the birth of her daughter, even though they'd just met! Reunited six months later, attraction flares into passion. Her independence is everything, but the offer of love and a father for Emma seems tantalisingly close…

THE OUTBACK NURSE *by Carol Marinelli*

In isolated Kirrijong, Sister Olivia Morrell had her wish of getting away from it all, and Dr Jake Clemson suspected that she had come to the outback to get over a broken heart. If she had to learn that not all men were unreliable, could he be the one to teach her?

On sale 6th July 2001

Available at most branches of WH Smith, Tesco, Martins, Borders, Easons, Sainsbury, Woolworth and most good paperback bookshops 0601/03b

MILLS & BOON

0501/114/MB13

IN HOT PURSUIT

Nat, Mark and Michael are three sexy men, each in pursuit of the woman they intend to have...at all costs!

Three brand-new stories for a red-hot summer read!

**Vicki Lewis Thompson
Sherry Lewis
Roz Denny Fox**

Published 18th May

4 BOOKS
AND A SURPRISE GIFT!

We would like to take this opportunity to thank you for reading this Mills & Boon® book by offering you the chance to take FOUR more specially selected titles from the Medical Romance™ series absolutely FREE! We're also making this offer to introduce you to the benefits of the Reader Service.™ —

- ★ FREE home delivery
- ★ FREE monthly Newsletter
- ★ FREE gifts and competitions
- ★ Exclusive Reader Service discounts
- ★ Books available before they're in the shops

Accepting these FREE books and gift places you under no obligation to buy; you may cancel at any time, even after receiving your free shipment. Simply complete your details below and return the entire page to the address below. *You don't even need a stamp!*

YES! Please send me 4 free Medical Romance books and a surprise gift. I understand that unless you hear from me, I will receive 6 superb new titles every month for just £2.49 each, postage and packing free. I am under no obligation to purchase any books and may cancel my subscription at any time. The free books and gift will be mine to keep in any case.

MIZEC

Ms/Mrs/Miss/Mr ....Initials ....
BLOCK CAPITALS PLEASE

Surname ....

Address ....

....

....Postcode ....

Send this whole page to:
UK: FREEPOST CN81, Croydon, CR9 3WZ
EIRE: PO Box 4546, Kilcock, County Kildare (stamp required)